D0122466

SPIRIT HUNTERS

ELLEN OH

SPIRIT HUNTERS

HARPER
An Imprint of HarperCollins*Publishers*

Spirit Hunters

For information address HarperCollins Children's Books, a division of HarperCollins Publishers, 195 Broadway, New York, NY 10007.
www.harpercollinschildrens.com

Library of Congress Control Number: 2016961854
ISBN 978-0-06-243008-3

Typography by Andrea Vandergrift
17 18 19 20 21 CG/LSCH 10 9 8 7 6 5 4 3 2 1

First Edition

To my dad, the ultimate storyteller.
I miss your stories.

SPIRIT HUNTERS

A NEW FRIEND

Day 1–Monday morning

"Harper! Come quick!"

Harper Raine looked up from unpacking her books to see her four-year-old brother, Michael, in her doorway. He could hardly stand still, hopping on one leg and then the other. She wiped the sweat beading on her forehead and fanned herself with the book she was holding.

"Little dude, the bathroom's across the hall," Harper said, turning back to fill her bookshelves.

"I don't have to pee! I just want you to come to my room. Hurry up!" Michael said. He ran in and grabbed her by the hand, trying to pull her onto her feet.

Deliberately making herself heavy, Harper slumped down and placed a little of her weight on his shoulders.

"All this unpacking and moving is exhausting," she said. "Maybe you should carry me on your back."

"Okay, Harper, I'll help you," he said, his little feet sliding around on the wooden floors. With a loud grunt, her brother pulled harder, trying to move them as quickly as he could.

After a long moment, Harper smothered a smile and relented. She straightened up with a big stretch. "That helped a lot! Thanks, buddy!"

He grabbed her by the hand again. "Let's go!"

The hallway was even hotter than her room and Harper cursed their new but ancient house for the millionth time. There was a reason it had been abandoned for over twenty years. It was a wreck. When their parents had decided to relocate to Washington, D.C., they'd bought it because of its "gothic charm." Harper still couldn't figure out the charming part. One year of renovations and the house was still not ready, but it hadn't kept their parents from moving the whole family down from New York City in the height of the summer.

Michael seemed unaffected by the heat, rushing her down to the other end of the corridor. His room was the first that they'd unpacked so there were no boxes. It was bright and airy with three large windows that faced the front. Everything had been neatly organized and arranged by their mother and father. Harper was bummed that twelve was deemed old enough to unpack her own room. The only thing worse than unpacking was packing in the first place.

As she stepped in, she couldn't help but notice how much cooler his room was. Puzzled, she sat on the edge of his bed, discomfited by the unnatural chill.

"What are you so excited about?" she asked, ignoring the creepy-crawly sensation that sent a shiver down her back.

"My new friend, Billy," he said, pointing to the corner where his large toy chest sat.

Harper gazed at the corner, and the hairs on the back of her neck began bristling. There was a sudden distortion in the air, and her vision blurred. And then nothing. She gave her brother a quizzical look.

"You can't see him?" Michael looked crushed.

He turned and stared at the toy chest again and then nodded. "Billy said you have to be special to see him. I guess you're not special," he said sadly.

His words triggered a sudden memory. Harper was five years old trying to introduce her best friend to her older sister, Kelly.

"I'm telling Mom that you're making stuff up!"

"I'm not! She's right there. Why won't you believe me?"

There was a loud humming in her ears and she could feel the beginning of a migraine throbbing in her right temple. She took a deep breath and focused on her brother. But before she could speak, there was a knock at the door and their mother, Yuna, appeared.

"Michael, you can't leave your toys out in the hallway," she said. "Somebody could trip and hurt themselves on them."

In her hands, she held a beat-up old-fashioned red fire truck. It was completely made of metal and looked like an antique. The paint was a dull red, chipped and faded. On the side of the long wagon, it said "City Fire Department" in gold paint. There were two ladders on either side of the truck, with a pulley and a crank to hoist them up, and a little brass bell hanging from the front of its engine.

"But that's not mi—" Michael stopped short. "Oh. That's Billy's!"

"Who's Billy?"

"He's my best friend," Michael said. "He lives in the house."

As a look of puzzled alarm spread over their mother's pretty face, Harper jumped to her feet with an overly loud laugh.

"We were just playing a game," Harper said. "You know, making up stories about people who lived here before. Right, Michael?"

Harper turned her back to her mother quickly as she faced Michael. She pressed her finger to her lips, her eyes growing big as she gestured for him to be quiet.

Michael laughed. "Harper, you're so funny."

Harper grabbed her little brother and swung him onto his bed, tickling him into a fit of giggles. She stole a glance at her mother, noting that her expression had relaxed a little.

"All right, next time be more careful," Yuna said. She placed the truck on the nightstand and walked out.

Harper heaved a sigh of relief and collapsed on the bed. Michael climbed on top of her and sat on her stomach.

"Why didn't you want me to tell Mommy about Billy?" he asked.

A rising nervousness made Harper's stomach clench as she pictured her mother's look of disappointment.

"Mom doesn't like things she doesn't understand," she said.

"Because she can't see him, either?"

"Yeah," Harper said. From the corner of her eye, she thought she saw a movement. She looked around the room in confusion. Her head throbbed.

"That's okay, as long as I can see him," Michael said. He hopped off the bed.

Reaching for his Lego box, Michael dumped all the contents onto his carpet and sat down.

"Come on, Billy, let's play!"

Harper was walking over to the door when Michael stopped her.

"Hey, Harper, wait. Billy said don't go up into the attic."

"Why?"

Michael shrugged. "He just doesn't want anyone up there."

"Well, I don't think Mom and Dad plan on touching the attic for a while," Harper said. "They're focused on fixing the central air-conditioning and everything else that's wrong with this stupid house."

The spotty air-conditioning was their first priority.

They'd only been in Washington, D.C., for two days and were already suffering from the heat and humidity. Yet Harper found it odd that the old house was strangely cold in certain spots. Like Michael's room.

Michael stopped playing with his Lego toys and looked up at Harper with a serious expression.

"Billy doesn't like it when you call his house stupid," he said.

"Well, it's not his house, it's *our* house," she retorted.

"No, Harper, this is Billy's house. He's one of the people who lived here before us."

The cold in the room deepened, causing goose bumps to spread all over her arms and back. Harper fumbled for the doorknob. She was desperate to get away.

Back in her room, Harper felt warm and clammy, as if she was running a fever. She welcomed the heat that she'd been cursing only a few minutes earlier. At least it was normal. Her head still pounded, and she knew if she didn't take something, the migraine would overwhelm her. She rifled through her bag and pulled out the little pillbox that her mom refilled every day. All other medicines in the house were kept locked in the medicine cabinet. After swallowing some ibuprofen, Harper continued unpacking.

While sorting her books onto her shelves, she came upon a small photo album. Her mother had given it to her as a memory book when they were packing to leave New York. Harper had barely glanced through it before, but now she sat down on her unmade bed and flipped it open. Each photo was methodically labeled with the date and Harper's age. It was typical of her mother, who was a corporate lawyer and notorious for her meticulousness. There were a few baby pictures, which Harper paged through. She smiled at seeing her two-year-old self eating spaghetti for the first time and a photo of her at four underneath the *T. rex* exhibit at the Museum of Natural History. She was making a scary face at Kelly, her older sister, who stood there looking bored. Seeing those early pictures again, she felt like she was looking at a finished jigsaw puzzle that had one obvious missing piece. No matter how you stared at it, you couldn't help but be aware of the gaping hole in the middle. The trouble was, Harper couldn't put her finger on what the missing piece was.

And that wasn't all. Nothing had been the same since the accident. She just didn't feel like herself anymore. Harper turned the pages, trying to ignore her aching head. The more she thought about her missing memories, the worse she felt. All she knew were facts: the ones her parents relayed to her. Last fall, there was a fire at school, she was hospitalized, and had a terrible accident. But she had no recollection of what had happened to her.

In her photo book she found a picture of herself lying in a hospital bed with two arm casts. Kelly was holding a cake in front of her, which Michael was trying to eat with his entire face. It was her twelfth birthday. Halloween. In the picture, she was smiling, but her eyes looked haunted.

Harper absently rubbed both her forearms. The casts had been removed six months ago and the doctor had warned her of "phantom pains" in her injured areas. But she didn't have pain as much as the odd sensation that her casts were still on her arms.

Two badly fractured arms, a broken collarbone, several broken ribs, and no memory. Whatever had happened, Harper figured it must have been so bad that her mind had repressed the memories. Did she really want to remember them now?

HARPER'S STUPID DC JOURNAL

Entry #1

Things I hate:

1. *Our new/old house*
2. *Talking about my feelings*
3. *Washington, D.C.*
4. *Writing in this stupid journal*

The only reason I'm writing in here is because my therapist said it'll help regain my memories. She said now that I'm in Washington, D.C., I need to write everything down since I won't be able to see her anymore and it'll take time to find a new therapist. To be honest, I'm really not looking forward to that. I really like Julie a lot. What if I don't find a therapist I like as much? How'm I supposed to share my deepest private thoughts? It's not like I enjoy therapy all that much, anyway. It can be pretty boring at times.

At least no one will be looking at this but me, so I can use different color ink and doodle all over the pages. My sister, Kelly, would say that this is a waste. She disapproves of paper. She lives her life online for everything. Before we moved to D.C., there was a week where she went around telling everyone how paper was dead. It got to be so annoying that I went into the bathroom that she'd claimed for herself and took out all the toilet paper. On the mirror, I wrote in her red lipstick, "Paper is Dead." She hasn't bothered me since, but she does like to glare disapprovingly whenever she sees me using my notebook.

I don't really care what she thinks. I love paper. I love the feel of it when I'm writing or drawing on it and I love the smell of it when I open a brand-new journal. But mostly because if this journal helps me regain my memories, then I have to do it. I'll do anything to get rid of the empty feeling that comes with no memory. Sometimes I'll panic without even knowing why. I hate it! So I'm writing in this dumb journal. I just hope it helps.

THIS OLD HOUSE

Day 1–Monday afternoon

Late in the afternoon, Harper lay on the floor of her sweltering room fanning herself with a pretty folding fan that opened to a picture of a blossoming cherry tree. Her migraine had gone away, but she was still surrounded by boxes and she had no energy to unpack. The only things she'd managed to put away were her clothing and all her precious breakables: her prized *Totoro* and *Spirited Away* character figurines from Studio Ghibli and a black lacquered jewelry box with a butterfly design in mother-of-pearl that her grandmother had brought back from Korea.

She'd piled her long, thick, dark-brown hair

loosely on the top of her head but still sweat trickled down her neck.

"I hate this place."

She longed for the air-conditioned luxury of her old New York City apartment. Summer might be unbearably hot in New York, but there were plenty of places you could duck into for some cold, refreshing air-conditioning. Here in their Washington, D.C., neighborhood, the closest store was over two miles away and it was just too hot to walk. Her older sister had her driver's license but probably wouldn't want to go out. She was too busy chatting online with her friends. Harper could only hope one of her parents would stop unpacking and head out to the mall. She closed her eyes and thought of all things cold: Lying facedown on an ice-skating rink; sticking her head in the freezer; eating a cold, sweet ice . . .

"Ice cream! Who wants to go for some ice cream?" a voice hollered.

Harper's eyes flew open in amazement. *Wow, I'm good*, she grinned.

"Harper! Come on!" shouted Michael as he thundered down the stairs squealing ecstatically. Harper shook herself from her thoughts and dragged herself off the floor.

In the hall, her sister's door opened, letting out a

cool draft from the electric fan blowing in her room.

"Hey!" Harper glared in disbelief. "How come you got a fan in your room and I don't?"

She started to walk into Kelly's room but was blocked when Kelly closed the door behind her.

"I have a fan because I'm studying for the SATs, doofus," Kelly said. "Don't even think about going into my room."

Without moving from her position in front of her door, Kelly shouted, "Mom, can you get me a Mocha Frappuccino?"

As soon as she heard an affirmative, Kelly went back into her room and slammed the door. With an aggravated sigh, Harper stomped down the stairs.

"Mom, it's not fair! You and Dad have a ceiling fan in your room. Michael's room is cool, and now Kelly has her own fan," she whined. "It is so hot in this house! Why can't I have one, too?"

"You can sleep with me in my room, Harper," Michael said. "I don't mind."

"No way," she said, ruffling his hair. "You sleep like a wild man. I'd be one big bruise by morning." Not to mention how weird the abnormal chill in his room was—no way was she sleeping in there.

As she came downstairs, her mother was checking her face and hair in the elaborate gold-framed mirror in their foyer. Harper always felt like a circus elephant compared to her mother's petite gracefulness. It didn't help that Kelly was Yuna's clone. At twelve, Harper was already four inches taller than her mother and her older sister. She glanced for a brief moment into the foyer mirror, reaffirming once again that she looked nothing like her mother. Her face was round, not oval, her dark hair was wavy, her cheeks covered in freckles instead of being smooth and clear. The one thing she did inherit was her mom's narrow, monolid eyes, only without her mom's long full lashes. Even when she smiled, all she ever heard was that she was cute, not beautiful like they were. Not that she cared.

Just then a creepy sensation coursed down her spine, causing her to shudder. She had the oddest feeling. As if someone was watching her. She looked up toward the stairs, almost expecting to see someone peering over the banister at her. There was no one there, but the feeling remained. She backed up until she was right next to the foyer mirror and reached out to put her hand on the ornate gold frame. There was something comforting about the antique mirror. It had been in their family for as long as she could remember. When her mother had considered exchanging it for something more modern, Harper had panicked, refusing to give it up. She'd asked to hang it in her room but her parents had said no. So it hung in their new foyer, just like it had in their old apartment. It was something familiar that Harper could still rely on. Like now. She could feel the weird sensation fading as she clung to the mirror.

Finally done primping, Yuna hustled them out the front door and to the driveway where a silver minivan was parked.

"Mom, did you hear me?" Harper asked. "I really need a fan!"

"Oh, honey, I'm sorry, but if we put a fan in your room it would probably trip the circuit breakers," Yuna said. "The electrician and the air-conditioning repairmen will be here tomorrow. Hopefully you won't even need a fan once everything is fixed."

Her mother ignored her sullen look as she urged Harper and Michael into the minivan.

"If it gets too bad, you can sleep on the sofa downstairs. It's a little cooler there," her mother replied.

"Oh great, another sweaty miserable night. I hate this house," Harper fumed as she helped her brother buckle up. She was never allowed to have anything for herself.

Michael patted her hand in sympathy. "It's not so bad," he said. "And now we have lots of room!"

The old house was huge compared to their three-bedroom apartment in Manhattan. And it was nice to have her own bedroom and not have to share with Kelly, but Washington was entirely different from New York. The metro system was nowhere near as good as the New York subway. Also, people said "good morning" to you on the streets and expected you to chat with them. It was so weird.

No, she didn't like Washington. The only thing she liked about the move was being closer to her grandmother. She hadn't seen her in person since she was seven years old. But she always talked to her on the phone on her birthday, Christmas, and New Year's, and exchanged letters with her during the year. Her Grandma Lee was not much of a phone talker, but loved to send cards and little presents.

"When do we get to see Grandma?" Harper asked.

Their mother backed out of the driveway and onto the road. Harper could see her lips tighten in the rearview mirror.

"I don't know, we're a bit busy right now," Yuna said.

"I want to see Grandma!" Michael shouted excitedly. "I've never seen her. I only talked to her on the phone."

"Not right now," Yuna responded.

Harper sighed loudly. Just the other night she'd overheard her father telling her mom that she needed to make her peace with Grandma Lee now that she lived so close by.

"Well, can we call her and tell her we're here?" Harper asked.

"Drop it, Harper!" Yuna snapped.

The car quickly became quiet. Harper glanced at Michael, who was sticking out his lower lip in a pout.

"Mommy, does Grandma not want to see me?" he asked in a quivering voice.

Their mother ran a hand through her hair, clearly trying to control her temper.

"No, honey, that's not it at all," Yuna said with a sigh. "She loves you. It's about my relationship with her. We don't agree on anything."

Before Michael could ask any more questions, Harper shook her head at him. Their mom looked sad and angry. But it was Michael that Harper felt sorry for.

Harper didn't know why it was that Grandma Lee stopped visiting. But she at least remembered when they used to see Grandma Lee often. Harper knew how much fun Grandma was. When Harper was younger, Grandma used to come once a month to cook Korean food and buy them special treats from the Korean market. It had been five years since Harper had last seen her grandmother, but she could still picture her vividly. She could see Grandma's bright happy smile, the way her eyes crinkled tight at the corners. The way she always smelled of oranges.

She remembered being told that traveling was getting hard for Grandma. But then she'd stopped visiting on Christmas also, and Harper realized that her mother and grandmother had had a big falling out. When she'd asked Kelly what had happened, Kelly had said, "It's because of you . . . it's *always* because of you."

Harper shivered at the memory. It had upset her so much that she'd never asked anyone about it again. Not even her grandma.

As their minivan pulled into the parking lot of the local supermarket, Harper sighed with disappointment.

"What's wrong now?" her mom asked, sounding annoyed again.

"Nothing," Harper said. She was bummed her mother hadn't taken them to the mall instead. It would have been nice to walk around a cool place and just people-watch. It was one of her favorite pastimes when she'd lived in New York. You could be anywhere in the city and find interesting people to gawk at.

Inside, Harper shuffled slowly down the aisles, bored with suburbia, then almost bumped into an old lady. Harper stared. The woman's skin was nearly translucent and she had brassy yellow hair, which matched her yellow horselike teeth.

"What are you looking at?" the old lady groused at her. "Such a rude thing."

Shocked, Harper didn't know how to respond.

"What's the matter? Don't you speak English?"

"Of course I do," Harper replied indignantly.

"Where are you from?"

"From New York . . ."

"No, no, no, where are you really from? Where are your parents from?" the old lady badgered.

Harper had been taught to always respect her elders, but she could feel herself getting angry. Harper knew exactly what the old lady wanted to know. She was angling to find out what foreign country she was from. She'd heard this question many times before and it always upset her. It made Harper feel like she didn't belong.

"My father was born in Queens, New York, and my mother was born in Maryland," Harper shot back.

"What, are you adopted?"

"No. I was born here. We're Americans."

"Not with that face you're not," the old lady said.

Harper felt as if she'd been slapped. Anger raged through her. But before Harper could yell at the old lady and call her a racist, her mother appeared, holding Michael's hand.

"What seems to be the problem?" Yuna asked, putting a calming hand on Harper's back.

"Now you, I can tell, are Chinese," the old lady replied. "I don't know why you Chinese people can't teach your children better manners. We don't stare in this country. It's rude."

"I'm not Chinese," Yuna replied in a mild manner. "I'm actually Korean, and I'm sorry if my daughter did anything to offend you. She is very well mannered and would never be rude on purpose." Yuna gave the old lady a sharp glance. "Unless she'd been provoked."

"What are you implying?"

"Have a nice day," Yuna cut her off and quickly led Harper and Michael into another aisle.

When they were safely away, Yuna let Harper go. "You okay, honey?"

Harper was still upset. "I've never had an old person be racist to me before."

Her mother's face looked sad. "They come in all

shapes, sizes, colors, and ages," she said. "But don't let them hurt you. That's giving them power that they don't deserve."

"She said I couldn't be American with a face like mine."

"She's just jealous of your beauty," her mother said, as she reached over to grab Harper by the cheeks and kiss her nose.

"Yeah, Harper, you are beautiful!" Michael said. "And that old lady wasn't."

"Michael," Yuna chided. "That's not nice."

"Well, she was mean to Harper! And I don't like her," he said folding his arms. "Besides, she had yellow teeth and bad breath."

"Michael," Yuna said in a stern voice. But Harper could see she was trying not to laugh.

Harper had to smile at her little brother's earnestness. She could feel her anger and hurt dissipate as she listened to his endless chatter. Fifteen minutes later, they carted their Popsicles and groceries to the car and headed home.

When they got there, Michael made a beeline for his bedroom, with Harper following slowly behind. As soon as he entered his room, he began talking to his imaginary friend. Harper took the last bite of her Popsicle and she lingered outside his open door, listening uneasily to his conversation. Suddenly he was quiet and when he spoke again, his voice was lowered, as if worried. Harper leaned closer.

"I'm sorry I didn't get you one. You want some of mine? I can share."

There was a slight thudding sound and then Michael cried out in dismay.

"What'd you do that for?"

Harper quickly ran into the room and saw Michael picking up the pieces of his Popsicle. It had been smashed, and his lips were quivering as he tried to clean up the blue stain that was spreading on his rug.

"What happened?" Harper asked. She grabbed some tissues and began to wipe up the mess.

"Billy is mad because I didn't bring him a treat," Michael said. "He knocked mine on the rug and said that now we both don't get any."

Harper would have laughed if Michael hadn't looked so upset. It was a pretty creative excuse for dropping a Popsicle.

"Well, that's a rotten thing for him to do," Harper said. "Tell you what, let's go downstairs and eat another one on the porch."

Michael shook his head sadly. "I don't feel like it anymore. I need to stay and play with Billy."

Harper froze at his words, gooseflesh rising across her arms. A wisp of a memory floated through her head, but she couldn't catch the details. Whatever it was, it made her uneasy. Leaning over, she picked Michael up and swung him around.

"Oh yeah? I don't think so! I want another Popsicle, and I need a good reason to get one. You're my excuse!" Harper carried him out into the muggy hallway.

Giggling, Michael wriggled out of her arms and ran down the stairs first.

"I'm gonna beat you!" he shouted.

As Harper began to follow him, Michael's door slammed shut abruptly. Harper stared at his room in shock.

"It was probably just a draft or these shaky wooden floors," she said to herself. "Stupid old house."

Suppressing a shudder, she hurried away, afraid to look behind her.

HARPER'S STUPID DC JOURNAL

Entry #2

Things I hate:

1. *D.C. is way too hot and humid.*
2. *No stores close enough to walk to*
3. *This house is so old and creepy, and it smells bad sometimes.*
4. *Nightmares*

Ever since moving here, I've been having awful nightmares. They're so vivid and detailed. I can feel myself thinking and acting and moving in such a real way. But it's just in my head, right?

Sometimes, I'm not even sleeping. I'm just kind of sitting there and all of a sudden I'm in a dream. It's like watching a horror movie where the character who you know is about to die next is heading toward the danger instead of running away like any smart person would do. And you can see their horrified expression as it dawns on them just how dumb they've been. I hate those movies. Fact—Real people run away from danger. But in my dream, I'm the one walking right into the monster's trap, and no matter how much I try I can't make myself stop. Except, the thing is, I never get to the end. I wake up right as I head into the darkness. Yeah, that's what my dreams are like. Super frustrating. I know that if I could just stay in the dream a little longer, I'd find out what happened to me at Briarly and then I could stop writing in this stupid journal. No offense, journal.

It's just that trying to remember is like swimming through Jell-O. My memory is cloudy and messed up. I'm not sure what's real and what's my imagination. What's fact and what's fiction.

Fact—There was a fire at my old school.

Fact—I got sent to Briarly, a mental health institute for children in New York.

Fact—A terrible accident happened there that left me with two broken arms, a broken collarbone, and several broken ribs.

Fiction—I hurt myself.

I remember the police coming and asking me lots of questions that I couldn't answer. It was the police officer who told me how Briarly claimed they had done nothing wrong and that I must have done this to myself. But the police officer said that it was impossible. Emergency room doctors examined my injuries and concluded that "they could have only been sustained by a great fall or violent trauma." Whatever that means. To make things worse, the surveillance video for the night was filled with static and glitches. The only person who knows what happened to me that night is me—and I can't remember anything.

The doctors call it "dissociative amnesia." The trauma

to the head and the trauma of the event were too great for my brain to process. So I forgot it all.

My parents sued Briarly. The hospital administration didn't want to go to trial and so they gave me a lot of money in a settlement, which my parents put in something called a trust that's just for me. It's supposed to be enough to live on for the rest of my life.

But I think I'd rather have my memory back.

IN THE NEIGHBORHOOD

Day 2–Tuesday afternoon

Harper needed to get out. Her parents were going nuts dealing with the electrician, the plumber, and the air-conditioning men all trying to work at the same time. While her mother was usually a tense person, this was the first time Harper had ever seen her laid-back father get so frustrated. With both Michael and Kelly hiding out in their rooms, Harper was going stir crazy.

Even though it was sweltering outside, Harper figured it had to be better than the alternative. With everyone busy, it was easy to sneak into the garage, where she found her bike and helmet propped against a wall. It had been a while since she'd been for a ride.

As she was about to slide open the outer door, Harper heard something stir behind her, making her flinch. She hated that this house creeped her out so much.

"I spy a breakout in progress," boomed a man's voice.

Harper relaxed her shoulders and turned around. Her dad, Peter, was looking down at her with an amused glance. At six feet, he was the only one in her family who could still make Harper feel little. "I'll have to alert the warden that one of the prisoners is trying to escape."

"I thought I'd go for a ride around the neighborhood," Harper said. "I can't unpack anymore."

A sudden cold, sharp sensation on the back of her neck made Harper flinch again. Rubbing the now tender spot, she looked up to see her father's concerned glance.

"You okay, honey?" he asked. "Is anything hurting?"

Harper put down her hand and forced a smile. She knew her father was just worried about her old injuries. "I'm fine! I just need to get out."

Her father looked like he was going to question her some more, but then one of the contractors called for him to come over.

"You know the drill," he said to Harper. "Wear your helmet, be careful, keep your phone on, don't go too far, and be home in a couple of hours, deal?" He looked her straight in the eye.

Harper nodded and took off before he could talk to her mother and change his mind. Her parents had become super overprotective since her accident. It was Julie, her therapist, who'd reminded them that doing normal activities was an important part of the healing process. But her mom still liked to keep Harper home and safe whenever she could.

Outside, it had to have been a scorching ninety-five degrees with no cloud coverage in sight, but Harper didn't care. She felt free and relaxed, like she could breathe again. She was happy to be out and exploring the neighborhood. For a moment she toyed with the idea of looking for her grandmother's house but she didn't know how to get there. Plus, she knew her mother would probably kill her.

With a sigh, she headed to the nearby park. There were very few people around. One mother with her toddlers, and a guy walking his dog. Harper didn't see any kids her age so she kept riding. She remembered hearing that there was a library nearby. With only a vague idea of where it might be, she started down the street, screeching to a halt as a small white dog stopped in front of her, barking furiously.

"Pumpkin! Bad dog!" A short girl with brown skin and tightly braided hair snatched up the wriggly dog.

"Sorry about that," she said. "Pumpkin has this thing for people on bikes."

"Pumpkin?" Harper said in a disbelieving tone.

The girl rolled her eyes. "I know, silly, right? She's my grandma's dog. If it had been left to me I would have named her something that suits her, like Jerkface or Pain in My Butt."

Harper laughed. "I take it you don't like her very much." Pumpkin was wriggling out of the girl's arms, trying to avoid the leash. "Here, let me help you."

The girl gave her a grateful thank-you as Harper clipped on the leash and they could put the hyperactive dog down. Immediately Pumpkin ran around them, testing the limits of the retractable chain.

"It's not that I hate her," the girl said. "It's just that she is the most spoiled and worst-trained dog in the world so I hate taking care of her. But my grandma is on a ten-day cruise and I got stuck with her precious Pumpkin."

With a bright smile, the girl looked Harper over thoroughly. "My name is Dayo Clayton," she said. "I've never seen you around. Are you new?"

Harper nodded and introduced herself. "We just moved into the neighborhood."

"Where are you from?"

Harper tensed a little, wondering what she really meant by that.

"I'm from New York," she replied.

"New York City?"

Harper nodded.

"That's so cool. When I grow up I want to live there," Dayo said. "So what school are you going to?"

Harper relaxed and shrugged. "I don't know yet. But I'll be starting seventh grade."

"Me too! That means we'll both be going to Little Ridge Middle School, unless you go private."

Harper shook her head. "Nah, we're public school kids."

Dayo beamed happily and launched into a long explanation of what Little Ridge was like and who in their neighborhood attended.

Harper found herself liking her new friend very much. She liked the wide gap between Dayo's front teeth, which showed whenever she smiled, and she liked the freckles that covered her nose and cheeks. For the first time since moving, she felt a cautious hopefulness. They walked around the block as they talked, following Pumpkin, who clearly believed she was the leader. Thirty minutes passed as the girls chatted, until the little dog plopped down on the sidewalk, her tongue hanging out.

"I'd better get Jerkface home," Dayo said reluctantly. "I'm around the corner on Davenport. Where do you live?"

"We moved into the oldest house in the entire neighborhood. You know the one that looked like it should have been torn down ages ago?"

Dayo's warm brown eyes grew wide, and her freckles seemed to stand out in sharp relief. "Oh, so you're the family who's living in the old Grady house! We've all been wondering who bought that place. Is it really haunted?"

There was both admiration and fear in Dayo's voice. But Harper was more bothered by her words.

"What do you mean, haunted?"

"I mean that house has been empty for years. The reason it was abandoned for so long is because nobody has ever been able to live there." Dayo's eyebrows furrowed tightly in concern. "Rumor has it that Mr. Grady made a pact with the Devil to live forever but then he disappeared. No one knows what happened to him. But ever since then, there have been horrible things going on there. They say kids have died in that house."

"*Died?* How?"

"I don't know exactly," Dayo said. "All I know is that it was bad."

The hair on the back of Harper's neck felt electrified and it took all her willpower to suppress a shudder. She forced herself to laugh.

"That's crazy talk," she said. "They're just old stories to keep everyone away from the house."

"Well, they worked! Nobody ever goes near the Grady house."

"It's the Raine house now," Harper said. "You want to come over?"

Dayo looked torn, as if she wanted to say yes but was too scared to. "Sure, I'll ask my mom," she said after a while. "I've gotta go to my aunt's tomorrow. Every other Wednesday I babysit my baby cousin George while my aunt meets with her writing group." Dayo rolled her eyes. "My aunt wants to be a writer, but as far as I can tell, these meetings aren't for writing, they're for a whole lot of talking and eating! Anyway, they meet for hours so my mom drops me off at lunch and picks me up before dinner. The only good thing is that at least I get paid. But I'm free the rest of the week. I can come Thursday."

Harper nodded. "Yeah, just come on over. I'm not doing anything but unpacking the entire week." She pulled a face. "It's so boring and my room is really hot. I can't stand it."

"Why don't you come to my house right now?" Dayo said. "You can help me retrain Jerkface to understand what 'stay' actually means. Plus my mom's a caterer, and she makes the best cookies in the world."

With a grin, Harper followed Dayo to a pretty little white house that had a bright yellow door and blue shutters. She met Dayo's mother, a cheerful woman with thick, poufy hair that she had tied back with a colorful scarf. She looked almost identical to her daughter, right down to the profusion of freckles across their noses.

"You're the first friend of Dayo's who didn't need to be told to take off their shoes," Mrs. Clayton said with an approving smile, as Harper slipped her sneakers off in the foyer.

Harper smiled back. "My mom is Korean and she doesn't let anyone walk with shoes in the house. Especially because living in New York City, the streets are way dirtier than out here."

The Clayton house was bright and colorful and smelled of the most delicious aromas in the world. There were lots of things cooking. Harper could smell sweet cookies baking in the oven, as well as a rich savory meat stew that made her mouth water in hunger.

"What is that amazing smell?" she asked, closing her eyes as she took a deep whiff.

"That would be Jamaican oxtail stew, Dayo's favorite," Mrs. Clayton said. "I would give you some now but it's still a few hours from being ready. Would you like to stay for dinner?"

"You should stay," Dayo piped in. "My mom's oxtail stew wins all the prizes! She serves it over rice and peas and it is the best thing ever. Have you had oxtail before?"

Harper nodded. "I've had Korean oxtail soup, but it doesn't smell like this! I wish I could stay, but I have to be home for dinner."

"Next time, then," Mrs. Clayton said with a big smile. "But for now, why don't you dig into some of my special oatmeal, cranberry, and white chocolate cookies."

The intoxicating aroma of the cookies softened Harper's disappointment about not being able to stay for dinner. She sat eagerly at the table with Dayo and scarfed down the heavenly cookies, still hot from the oven. Mrs. Clayton poured out cold glasses of skim milk for the perfect combination.

"Mrs. Clayton," Harper said. "These are the best cookies I ever ate in my entire life."

"Told you my mom's the best chef in the whole world!" Dayo said proudly.

"You're so lucky, my parents almost never cook. And when they do, it's just boring stuff," Harper sighed.

"Well, now that you're here, you can come eat with us anytime!" said Dayo.

A rush of warmth filled Harper's heart with a sensation she only vaguely remembered feeling before. It was the realization that she had connected with a true friend.

Afterward, Harper enjoyed watching Dayo's frustration build as she tried to train Pumpkin on basic commands. "You're being too nice," Harper chimed in after the tenth time that Pumpkin ignored Dayo's commands. "She hears your sweet voice and assumes that she's the boss of you," Harper said. "Try being firm with her."

Dayo commanded Pumpkin to stay one more

time, but the dog still wouldn't listen. She threw up her hands. "I give up. You try."

Harper stood up tall and approached Pumpkin. In a loud, firm voice she told the dog to sit. Pumpkin sat. Dayo stared in awe.

"How did you do that?"

"She's smart enough to realize that I'm the boss of her," Harper said.

Dayo sighed. "Maybe it's 'cause you're tall and I'm short. Even my grandmother is short."

Harper shook her head. "It has nothing to do with size, it's all attitude. Like right now you should stand up really tall, look at me, and command me to sit."

Dayo's bright eyes grew round. "But . . ."

"Just do it, and be as tough as you can, but not mean."

Dayo jumped to her feet, pulled back her shoulders, and using her most forceful voice, commanded Harper. Harper immediately sat. So did Pumpkin.

"Now use that same voice with all your commands to Pumpkin," Harper said.

With newfound confidence, Dayo once again began to retrain Pumpkin. This time, the dog listened.

"This is awesome!" Dayo crowed in delight. "How did you know how to do all this? Do you have a dog?"

"No, I wish I had one. My dad is allergic and my mom doesn't like dogs. But my grandmother has a Yorkie named Monty," Harper said. "He's so well trained that you could put a stack of bacon in front of him and he wouldn't eat it until my grandma tells him he can."

"Wow, think Pumpkin could get that good?"

"Yeah, as long as you keep this up, you can train her. She's pretty smart for a dog named Pumpkin."

They both laughed.

"You know, it's too bad you don't have a dog," Dayo said.

"Why's that?"

"Because if your house is really haunted, a dog could help chase the ghosts away." Dayo grinned. "Maybe you can borrow Pumpkin for a day and go ghost hunting."

Harper smiled back. "I don't know who'd be more scared to see a ghost, me or Pumpkin."

Dayo giggled in agreement. But Harper's good mood had shifted. And as she thought of her new home, she felt like a dark cloud had parked itself above her. After a few more minutes, she headed home, biking the seven blocks quickly. Outside the house, she stood, taking it in. It looked different from the first time she saw it. The dingy gray exterior had been repainted a clean white, and all the shutters had been replaced. Even the roof was brand-new. But it still retained its sense of ancientness.

Just as she was about to head inside, she saw something flicker in the far right window. Someone was there, but all she could make out were dark eyes set against ghostly pale skin. She rubbed her eyes and looked again, but the figure was gone.

It was Michael's window.

HARPER'S STUPID DC JOURNAL

Entry #3

Things I hate:

1. *The weird cold spots in this house*
2. *The weird warm spots in this house*
3. *The weird smells in this house*

This house creeps me out so bad. It makes me feel like I'm suffocating. I don't get how nobody else can feel it.

Fact—When I'm downstairs, I hate being alone anywhere except the foyer. It's the one spot that I can breathe normally in.

And like I said, there are so many strange pockets of cold and warm spots. In the far right corner of the dining room, there's a draft that my parents say is caused by the old ventilation system. But it doesn't feel like a regular old draft to me. It's cold and clammy, like when you've been running in the heat and then go into really cold air-conditioning. You still feel hot and sticky but you're also chilled from the cold. That's what it feels like. And every now and then there is this sweet and sickly odor of something dead.

Dad says that given how old the house is, many things have probably died here and left their bones decaying within the walls. That's just so gross.

And it's so much worse upstairs.

My room feels safe. But sometimes the bells on my doorknob will ring on their own. It makes me shudder, even though the ringing never lasts long. The bells hang above a bright-red Korean purse with a gold embroidered design.

Fact—Both are very special because Grandma Lee gave them to me when I was little. She made me promise to always hang them on the inside doorknob of my bedroom.

I miss her. She always made me feel loved and comforted. I guess that's why the bells and the little purse always make me feel safe. Although, I don't know why. I once peeked into the pouch and I'm pretty sure that the only thing in it was salt, a weird hairy green leaf that I think is fennel, and pine needles. But I keep the purse and bells because they remind me of my grandma.

My favorite memory of Grandma Lee is when she taught me how to make homemade dumplings. It was so much fun. Spreading egg wash on the wrappers and spooning in the meat and veggie mixture. I overstuffed mine so that they broke completely apart when she fried them, but they still tasted good! I really can't wait to see my grandma!

Shoot. The bells are ringing again. It's as if someone is trying to get into my room but they can't get through my door. I don't know who it is and I don't want to know, either.

SO MUCH DRAMA

Day 2–Tuesday evening

"Dad, did you know that this house is supposed to be haunted?" Harper asked as she shoveled mashed potatoes onto her dinner plate.

Kelly rolled her eyes. "Please don't start. It'll be hard enough making new friends without you spreading stories again."

"I'm not! I just found out about it from a girl I met in the neighborhood," Harper said.

"Well, she's an idiot."

"No, she's not! Butthead!"

"Both of you stop it right now." Their mother's voice was loud as she put the salad bowl down hard enough to spill some tomatoes onto the table. Michael remained unusually quiet.

"We will not have such nonsense in this house. Do you understand me, Harper?"

"But it's not nonsense! This used to be called the old Grady house because Mr. Grady vanished and was never seen again . . ."

The moment Harper spoke, a sharp and sudden shiver ran through her. An eerie sensation nearly overwhelmed her, as if the house were waiting to hear what she would say next.

"I hate this house. It's so weird—"

"I said stop it!" Her mom's tone was razor-sharp with anger.

At that moment, Harper felt terribly lonely. She slouched in her seat and wondered why she was so different from the other members of her family. She suddenly missed her grandmother with a fierce ache.

"Are we ever going to see Grandma again?"

Her mother heaved a heavy sigh. "My mother is a very busy woman. As soon as we get more settled in, I'll see what we can schedule."

"She hasn't seen me since I was seven years old. Wouldn't she want to make time?" Harper asked. She noticed that even Kelly was looking up with curiosity at their mom.

"I'm just not ready for this right now, Harper, there's too much to do."

"I always thought Grandma didn't want to see us anymore, but I guess it's actually you that doesn't want to see her," Harper said.

"That's enough!" Yuna had reached her limit. Harper could tell from the tone of her voice that she'd gone too far. Tightening her lips, she slunk lower in her seat. Her father reached over to give her hand a sympathetic squeeze, but Harper pulled away, too upset to be consoled.

Kelly scowled at her before picking up her plastic fork and knife to cut into the roast beef. Before Harper could ask what Kelly was mad about, her sister's utensils snapped in half.

"Damn it! Why can't we use regular silverware like normal people!" This time there was no mistaking the anger Kelly was directing toward Harper.

"Why are you glaring at me? It's not my fault," Harper sputtered.

"Everything is your fault!" Kelly snapped. "Even us moving down here is all because of you!"

"Kelly!" There was a sharp warning in Yuna's voice that caused Kelly to clamp her lips together.

"What do you mean because of me?" Harper asked. "How could Mom and Dad opening up a law firm in Washington have anything to do with me?"

"Because you're so freaking weird, that's why!"

Peter rapped his knuckles hard on the table. "Stop it, girls. Our move here was for work, pure and simple. Now let's eat."

After a moment, Yuna started asking Kelly about her online SAT prep course, as if nothing unusual had occurred. While her sister began a litany of complaints, Harper stared at her plate, blinking back her angry tears. Kelly always blamed Harper for everything. Even using stupid plastic knives, which was clearly for Michael's sake, or so she'd thought. She couldn't remember when they'd begun to use them.

What did it matter, anyway? Her mother never yelled at Kelly. The perfect child that could do no wrong. While Harper could do nothing right. Her feelings were becoming harder to contain and she wanted to scream and throw her plate on the floor. She wanted to smash something. She wanted to see her mother's tight face go slack in shock. She wanted to show her just how angry she was. No longer hungry, Harper picked at the roast beef and pushed around her mashed potatoes and salad, making it look as unappetizing as possible.

"Harper, if you're not going to eat, then you are excused from the table," said Mom.

Harper bit down hard on her lip, and tasted her own blood. She stood up abruptly and grabbed her plate. After scraping it off in the garbage, she left it in the sink and stormed off to her room.

On her bed, she kicked and punched and screamed into her pillow until the rage died down. This was not a new feeling. Every once in a while, Harper would fall into an unexplainable funk that would leave her sad and angry. She felt like a piece of her was missing—a piece she couldn't explain.

There was a knock on the door and her father poked his head in with two bowls of strawberry ice cream. "How are you, sweetie?"

Harper heaved herself up and plopped onto the floor. Her father sat down next to her and passed her one of the bowls.

"Dad, what happened between Grandma and Mom? What did they fight about?"

He paused midbite. Putting down his bowl, he put a comforting arm around her shoulders.

"Both your mom and your grandma are very proud people with strong beliefs," he said. "And sometimes those beliefs clash."

"Their beliefs are more important than us?" Harper asked. "Grown-ups don't make any sense sometimes."

Peter laughed. "Yeah, we really don't. But your mom is working on it. Now that we live so close, she's willing to reach out to your grandma, but on her own terms and on her own schedule. Okay, champ?"

Harper nodded reluctantly and quickly polished off her ice cream. After her father left, she sat feeling sad and frustrated. Like she was in a dark place with no light to guide her out.

Something flickered in the periphery of her vision. She jumped to her feet and spun around, but there was nothing there. And yet it almost felt like someone was in her room. She heard the soft whisper of her name. It sent a chill down her spine. The strange, heavy, eerie feeling that had been with her during dinner was back again, pressing upon her. Glancing toward the door, she noticed that it was slightly ajar. Panicked, she slammed it shut. Immediately the sensation disappeared. She slid her body down to the floor, and rested her head against the door. Her grandmother's pouch and bells hung right next to her cheek. She pressed her face against them with a relieved sigh.

She needed to talk to someone. Anyone. For a brief moment she thought about calling Julie, her old therapist. But what could Julie do? She'd already told

Harper's parents she would have to find a new therapist in D.C.

With a deep sigh she pulled out her journal to write, but after a few minutes her head began pounding like a jackhammer inside her skull. Her migraine was back and the pain was blinding. Swallowing down her nausea, Harper crawled into bed and willed herself to sleep.

HARPER'S STUPID DC JOURNAL

Entry #4

Things I hate:

1. *Kelly*
2. *Migraines*
3. *Pigeons*

I miss New York. Well, except for the pigeons. I think they are the most disgusting creatures in the entire world. Every New Yorker I know refers to them as rats with wings. They are horrible and they aren't afraid of anything. I used to have nightmares about pigeons flying straight at my face and pecking my eyes out.

Last night I had this weird dream that I'd never had before. It was almost like a movie playing right in my head. A horror movie.

Fact or fiction—Was it a memory or a dream?

I don't really know because it felt very real.

In the dream it's nighttime and I'm all alone in a small ugly yellow room that I've never seen before. I know it's a hospital room, because it smells and looks like one. But it's weird because the only things in the room are a bed and a nightstand. The door's locked and there's only one large barred window, which is gross because the top half of it is covered in bird poop. The white sheets on the bed are thin and rough and cold. The only nice thing in the room is my brown fleece blanket I brought from home. I wrap myself in the blanket and huddle up tight against the wall.

There's nothing to do but stare at the patterns of crud on the window. There must be hundreds of pigeons roosting right above my window because I've never seen so much bird poop in my life. I can see the shadows of the birds moving about in the moonlight. They're cooing and fluttering their wings and making such a racket. They're taunting me because they're free, while I watch them from behind the bars of my window.

Bars. Like a prison. It's ironic. They must be thinking, Look at the human locked in the cage while we fly free and poop all over her window. *Stupid birds.*

The hospital staff treats me like a prisoner. Everything I brought from home is taken away from me. My books, my games, even my chocolate Pepero cookie sticks.

Fact—I love chocolate Pepero cookie sticks.

They said it was to keep me safe. Apparently cookies are dangerous. Maybe they thought I'd poke myself in the eye with one.

It doesn't matter. I couldn't eat anything, anyway. I have no appetite. I have no feeling except for the taste of fear in my mouth.

Fact—Fear has a taste. It tastes like blood.

The birds have all grown so quiet. I would have thought it was strange except I know that this is a bad thing. The temperature in my room has dropped so much I can't feel my toes and my breath is fogging up.

Someone's in my room.

And I'm so scared I can't breathe.

SOMETHING WICKED

Day 3–Wednesday morning

Harper threw down her journal with a sigh. She didn't want to think about her nightmares anymore. Even in the bright sunlight, the mere thought of them frightened her.

She looked around her room at the mess of boxes that still needed to be unpacked and she wanted to bury herself under her covers. The restless night made her tired and cranky and unwilling to work.

On her nightstand, there was a pink peony in a cup of water. Harper loved peonies. One of the few things she liked about their new house was the great big peony bushes in the back. Her mother must have brought the blossom up as a peace offering. She knew they were her favorites. Harper smiled, feeling the anger from the night before begin to dissipate.

Unwilling to write anymore, she decided to go check on Michael instead.

The air-conditioning was working and it was finally cool in the house, but as she approached Michael's room, Harper felt sweaty and clammy again. She hesitated at his door. It was completely silent in his room. Part of her was scared to go inside. It was like her nightmare, this feeling of unknown fear that made no sense. Shaking off her reluctance, she barged in. He was sitting in the middle of the room staring off into space. Even though the door slammed with a thud, he had no reaction. Harper knelt before him. His eyes were wide and unfocused. Whatever he was staring at was all in his head.

"Hey!" Harper grabbed him by the shoulders and shook him hard. "Snap out of it."

He blinked as his eyes focused. "Harper, what'd ya do that for?"

Relieved, she hugged him tight. "What were you looking at?"

Michael pushed away and looked all around the room. "You scared Billy off," he said. "He was going to show me a secret."

"What kind of secret?"

"He said he would come into my head and show me his memories," Michael said. "But you chased him away and now I don't get to see what they were."

An irrational terror struck Harper. She could feel the tight pull of anxiety around her chest as a sense of déjà vu assailed her.

Don't you want to see my secret, Harper? Just let me in and we'll be friends forever!

Harper gripped Michael tightly. "Michael, promise me you won't let him do that again."

"Why not?" Michael looked curiously at her.

"Because it's bad, really bad," Harper said. "Never do that again. Promise me."

Michael turned away to grab one of his toy cars. "Okay, I promise," he said. "Besides, I didn't like it at all. It made my head hurt real bad."

As Michael said this, the temperature inside the room dropped suddenly. "Why is it so cold in here?"

Michael looked at her in surprise. "It's not cold."

Harper pressed her lips tight to keep her teeth from chattering. Maybe she was getting sick and feverish. "Come on, let's go out to the park."

Michael hesitated. It looked like he was going to say no. He looked all around the room before nodding in agreement, and Harper hurried him out. She'd take the scorching heat of the park over the strange coolness in Michael's room any day.

Day 3–Wednesday evening

After a long afternoon running around outside and even getting their dad to drop them off at the movies, Harper and Michael were finally sitting in the living room watching TV.

Michael yawned and rubbed his eyes.

"Harper, I'm tired," he said.

"Hey, you wanna sleep in my room and have a mini campout?" Harper asked. The thought of Michael going back to his room bothered her.

"Yeah, but you still have boxes all over your floor!" Michael said. "Let's camp in my room instead."

"What about the living room? We can break out the sleeping bags and sleep down here," she said.

"Not tonight, honey," her father piped in from the adjacent dining room. "Your mom and I have some work to do down here."

Michael jumped to his feet and began to head upstairs. "It's okay, Harper," he said with another yawn. "We can do a campout another night."

She followed him upstairs and helped him wash up and change. As she sat next to him on his bed, the atmosphere of the room began to unnerve her. She didn't understand how Michael could fall asleep in such an uncomfortable place. Reluctantly, she exited the room and stood at the edge of the stairway. Harper didn't know what to do. She knew she couldn't tell her mother about Billy without making her freak out and overreact, and that was the last thing Michael needed, but she had to do something. She pressed her hands to her forehead. It felt like her brain was being ripped apart from the inside. She needed to have her mother refill her pillbox.

Then the whispering started again. The soft but panicked whispers of someone calling her name from a far distance. They hissed loudly in warning, and then a shout.

Suddenly, someone pushed her from behind. She could feel herself falling, her arms flailing as she tried to grab hold of the banister. Harper twisted her body into a ball as she crashed onto the steps; pain erupted as she slid down in rapid descent. It was only when she reached the first landing that she hit a barrier. Gasping in relief, Harper grabbed on to the wood slats of the railing, stopping her fall. She could swear that something had blocked her from plunging down to the bottom of the stairs, but when she looked to see what it was, there was nothing there.

What was going on? At the top, she'd felt two distinct hands pushing her hard. Now, she was stopped by an invisible barrier. Was she going crazy? She lay on the landing, trying to assess the damage and wondering what was happening to her, when her parents came running over.

"Harper!"

Her father reached her first, carefully checking out her limbs and asking where she was hurt. Her mother ran up right behind him, grabbing Harper's hand in a death grip.

"Harper? Harper? Talk to me, honey! Can you talk?" Yuna turned to Harper's father with a panicked look on her face. "I told you these stairs were too slippery. She could have been killed!"

From upstairs, Harper heard her sister gasp in shock.

"Is she okay?"

With everyone asking her if she was all right, Harper could only nod in dazed confusion. "My whole body hurts," she whispered.

Kelly walked carefully down the stairs in her bare feet.

"It's 'cause she was wearing socks," Kelly said. "Harper, you have to wear slippers or bare feet. The wood's too slick."

"Peter, I told you we should've put a runner on these stairs," Yuna fumed.

Harper's father nodded. "I'll take care of it first thing."

He leaned back and gave Harper a reassuring smile.

"Well, the good news is that you didn't break anything," her father said. "The bad news is that you are going to feel awful for a few days."

Harper grimaced at his forced cheerfulness. She hated when he tried too hard to act like something wasn't a big deal. Once Kelly was sure Harper was all right, she ran back up to her room.

Yuna pulled Harper up, exclaiming over the numerous bruises that were already sprouting on Harper's arms and legs.

"What if she reinjured herself? Maybe we should take her to the emergency room to be safe," Yuna said.

"No!" Harper yelled. "I don't want to go to the hospital!"

Peter gave Harper a gentle pat on the back. "I don't think you have to go. I think you're going to be all right. It could have been a lot worse," he said. "We're really lucky you didn't fall all the way down."

He kept a firm grip around her waist as she hobbled down each step. Yuna dashed ahead.

"I'll go get some ice packs and ibuprofen," her mother called over her shoulder.

As she followed her dad's lead, Harper looked up to the top of the stairs. She couldn't help but notice that even with all the commotion, Michael had never come out of his room.

HARPER'S STUPID DC JOURNAL

Entry #5

Things I hate:

1. *Being so klutzy*

Fact—I've broken more bones and had more bruises than any other kid I know.

My sister said I'm like a magnet of bad feng shui. As if I'm supposed to know what that means. I think it means "bad fortune" in Chinese. I guess she's right. I always seem to have the worst luck. Who else gets sent to a hospital and then breaks both arms, a collarbone, and some ribs?

Fact—All my life I've been extremely accident prone.

When I was five I sprained my ankle running in the park. When I was six I tripped and fell flat on my face, knocking my front teeth out. Lucky they were my baby teeth. When I was seven I broke my toes by accidentally kicking a brick covered in snow. That was the same year I fell off my bicycle and had to get stitches in my head. When I was eight I dislocated my collarbone falling out of a tree. When I was nine I got a concussion and was knocked unconscious by books falling off the shelves at the library. When I was ten I sprained my wrist after a bad fall. And when I was eleven. Well, you know what happened then.

The kids at school used to call me the Walking Disaster and would run away from me as if my bad luck was contagious. I guess they were right.

THE EVIL WITHIN

Day 4—Thursday morning

Harper was dreaming again. She knew it because she was back in the hospital room with the gated window. Only it was very dark. No moonlight shone through the bars of her window.

Was this Briarly? The bars on the window made her think it must be. It had to be a memory. But of a different night because the birds weren't cooing or fluttering like last time. She couldn't see their shadows on the window. They weren't there. Where could they have gone?

Suddenly, the room turned freezing cold. Her terror was immediate. She knew she was no longer alone in her room. Curling into a tight ball, she covered herself with her blanket and pressed her face to her knees, desperately afraid to see who was in the room with her. Her entire body shook as the bone-chilling cold came closer. Maybe if she never opened her eyes, whoever was there would tire of her and go away.

Then the whispering started. Harper whimpered as she covered her ears with her blanket. It was no good. She couldn't tune it out. The whispering was in her head now.

Bad girl, such a bad girl.

Look what you did!

Bad girl, what a bad girl.

They're never gonna let you go home.

The ice cold was creeping into Harper's bones and she knew that whoever was there was standing next to her. Someone she didn't want to see. She cowered under her blanket when it was suddenly ripped out of her hands.

Harper woke up with a violent jerk. This was a continuation of the previous nightmare. But she didn't want to know who was in the room with her in her dream. The fear was too intense. Although she still didn't recall her stay at Briarly, she thought this dream was about her time there. But was it fact or fiction?

Just the thought of it brought about a pounding headache. Harper sat up and immediately felt all the aches and pains from the fall. She wanted to lie back in bed and rest, but hunger and thirst made her head downstairs.

In the kitchen, Michael was sitting at the table as their mother was rushing around, unpacking things.

Her mother immediately came over to check on Harper.

"I'm fine, just sore," Harper said, waving her mother away.

With a concerned look, Yuna set a toasted waffle and maple syrup in front of Harper along with a side of fruit.

"Let me know if you need anything else," she said as she returned to her unpacking.

Harper ate slowly, watching as Michael sat falling asleep in front of his cereal bowl.

"Hey," she said as she nudged him. "Wake up before you have Frosted Flakes all over your face."

Michael's eyes popped open, but they looked glazed over and tired.

"What's going on, little buddy?" Harper asked, noticing the dark circles under his eyes.

He swatted her hand away with an irritated glare. "I'm fine, leave me alone."

Alarmed, she pressed her hand to his forehead. "Are you sick?"

"Just leave me alone!" Michael slammed his spoon down on the table and stomped away, leaving his cereal untouched.

Harper sat staring in stunned confusion. This was so unlike Michael.

Yuna glanced up but continued unpacking. "He's just tired and cranky this morning."

Troubled by his behavior, Harper finished eating and went upstairs to check on him. At his door, she could hear him speaking to someone. Harper pressed her ear close to listen to what was happening.

"Billy, stop! I don't like it when you do that," Michael said. "It makes me feel sick."

There was silence for a long time.

"No! Don't make me do that again!"

Concerned, Harper knocked on the door and opened it. "Michael, who are you talking to?"

At first glance, he looked frightened. But in the next moment, his little face contorted in rage. So red and swollen that it didn't look like her brother's face at all.

"Get out!" he screamed. He jumped to his feet and punched her over and over in her stomach, shoving her out of his room. Harper stood gaping in the doorway. What was happening to her brother? She was so shocked that she didn't stop him as he slammed the door in her face. Her stomach hurt not only from the pummeling, but from the sick feeling of dread growing within.

She stood there for several minutes, trying to hear what was happening. But Michael was completely silent. It was as if he was standing on the other side of the door, waiting for her to go away.

Finally giving up, she walked across the hallway and knocked on Kelly's door. It took several minutes before her sister finally opened up.

"I'm doing my online prep class right now," Kelly snapped. "Can't it wait?"

Harper shook her head. "There's something wrong with Michael," she said. "He's acting really weird and not like himself."

Kelly rolled her eyes. "Look, we just moved to a brand-new city, leaving all our friends behind. If I weren't so stressed about studying, I would be acting out a lot also," she said. "Just leave him alone. He'll be fine." And with that, she closed the door.

Harper walked slowly down the stairs, trying to figure out what was wrong with her little brother. Was she making a big deal out of nothing? She didn't know.

When the bell rang later that morning, Harper was relieved and happy to see Dayo at the door, with

Pumpkin running in circles at her feet.

"Is this a good time to come over?" Dayo asked.

"Yep!" Harper said. "My dad had to go into the office, so you can bring Pumpkin in. My brother will love her."

When Dayo stepped into the house, the little dog ran straight over to the foyer mirror. Growling low in her throat, she began to bark.

"Pumpkin, quiet!" Dayo commanded as she picked up the little dog and stood in front of the mirror. The little dog whined and hid its face in the crook of Dayo's elbow.

Dayo's brown eyes had grown wide in alarm. "I don't know what's gotten into her. She's never done that before."

Harper rolled her eyes. "It's a really old mirror, but I know for a fact that it's not haunted."

"How do you know?" Dayo asked.

"Because we've had that mirror in my family since I was little."

"Oh," Dayo said with a relieved smile. At that moment, Yuna walked out of the kitchen.

"Hey Mom, this is Dayo and her grandma's dog, Pumpkin."

"It's so nice to meet you." Yuna smiled at Harper's

friend. "Please feel free to visit as much as you can! I'm so glad Harper's found a new friend in the neighborhood."

Pumpkin was curled up tight and quiet in Dayo's arms.

"She's so sweet," Yuna said, giving the little dog a soft caress. "She's housebroken, right?"

Dayo nodded fervently. "She may not be the best-trained dog in the world, but she doesn't have accidents inside, I promise."

Harper's mother nodded.

"Harper, don't forget that your dad is terribly allergic, so just don't take her into our bedroom," she said. "That way your father won't have an allergy attack tonight."

"We won't," Harper said as she led her friend up to her room.

"Oh, and there's lots of snacks in the pantry, help yourself," her mother called.

"Your mother's really nice," Dayo said once they got into her room.

Harper shrugged.

"She's all right," Harper mumbled.

Harper sat on the floor and gave Pumpkin a good rubdown, to the dog's delight. She was happy to see them again. She could feel some of her anxiousness leaving her as she talked to Dayo and listened to her trials of retraining Pumpkin.

"Watch what I taught Pumpkin to do. Dance, Pumpkin!" Dayo snapped her fingers, and the little dog leaped onto her back legs and did a cha-cha-cha step.

"No way!" Harper exclaimed. "That's brilliant!"

Dayo grinned broadly as she fed Pumpkin a little treat. "It's amazing how fast she learned that trick. I never realized how supersmart she is! I owe you big for teaching me that assertiveness tip. I did more research on the internet and now she really listens to me. Won't my grandma be so surprised?"

"You might not want to give her back," Harper said.

Her friend grimaced. "Nah, it's okay. My grandma doesn't live too far away so I can visit anytime. And besides, my mom says she's so impressed with me that I'm probably ready to get my own puppy now!"

"That is so cool!"

Hearing Dayo talk about her grandmother made Harper miss Grandma Lee even more. She wondered when she would be able to see her and her Yorkie, Monty, again. Sighing, she realized she'd missed what Dayo had said.

Dayo was chatting about the kind of dog she'd want to adopt and different names that she liked. As they talked, Harper spread her legs out on the floor, and Dayo stopped midsentence.

"Wow, look at your legs!" Dayo exclaimed, staring at the mass of black-and-blue bruises. "What happened?"

Harper told her about her fall but held back the rest. She knew she couldn't tell Dayo about the feeling of hands pushing her from behind, of the barrier stopping her fall. She still didn't know what to think of the ghostly hands. It must have been her imagination.

"You could have died," Dayo said. She was about to say something else but Harper cut her off.

"The house is not haunted."

Dayo pressed her lips together. "Okay, maybe it isn't haunted. Maybe it's just bad luck. Either way, you should get Father Hurley to come and bless the house."

"Father Hurley?"

Dayo nodded. "He's the head priest at Our Lady of Mercy."

"Oh, but we're not Catholic," Harper said.

Dayo shrugged. "Well, why don't we go get some holy water and sprinkle it around the house anyway? I bet it can't hurt."

Talk of holy water and hauntings was beginning to make Harper's head pound all over again. She rubbed her temple, willing the pain away.

"Let's go show Pumpkin to my little brother. He loves dogs."

Dayo agreed, letting Harper pick up Pumpkin. As they approached Michael's door, Pumpkin began to growl. When Harper went to knock, Pumpkin wriggled frantically.

"What is wrong with her?" Dayo grabbed her from Harper's arms just as Michael opened the door.

Pumpkin made a high-pitched yip and jumped out of Dayo's arms, running straight down the hallway and into the master bedroom.

"Pumpkin!" Dayo chased after her as Michael stepped into the hallway. His cold expression changed as he caught sight of the fleeing dog.

"Is that a puppy?" Michael asked as he ran after them.

Harper could hear Michael squealing in excitement as her friend introduced him to Pumpkin. It was great to hear him sound like himself again.

But Harper couldn't move—she remained frozen in place, staring into his room. There was something bad in there. Even Pumpkin had sensed it.

Just as she was about to turn away, a slight tinny sound caught her attention. It was the antique fire truck her mother had found out in the hallway. The little brass bell hanging on the front of its engine was ringing ever so slightly. Harper didn't realize she'd walked into the room to take a closer look until she heard the door slam shut behind her. She whirled around, her heart beating loudly in her ears. She stepped toward the door but then the red truck began to roll around her feet, pushed by unseen hands. Faster and faster it circled her, its little bell ringing furiously. Harper closed her eyes, willing the illusion away. This couldn't be happening. Was she dreaming? She opened her eyes and gasped at the aggressive movements of the little truck. Every time she tried to head for the door, it would race in front of her, nearly clipping her toes. Harper sobbed in fright as she backed away, her legs pressing against Michael's bed.

"Kelly!" Harper shouted, hoping her sister would come and save her.

One of the fire truck's metal ladders began to

lift up as it continued to circle around her. She was just about to jump on the bed when she felt small, cold hands grab her by the ankles and pull her back viciously. She fell forward and saw that the fire truck had come to a stop right in front of her, the sharp spokes of its ladder extended straight up, toward her chest. Frantic, Harper twisted away from the truck, the tip of the ladder scraping across her neck as she landed heavily on the back end of it. The edge of the truck sliced deep into her upper arm. She grabbed her arm, screaming. She could feel blood seeping through her fingers. Pulling her hand away, she saw that the wound was deep and gaping. Helpless and in shock, she lay on the floor weeping in pain. The fire truck lay motionless on its side.

The door burst open as Dayo and Michael ran in. Dayo gasped in horror and immediately raced downstairs, shouting for Harper's mom. The noise brought Kelly out of her room.

"What the heck is going on?" she shouted as she walked into Michael's room.

Harper could only sob in reply.

"Harper, what did you do?"

Kelly ran out and raced back with a towel, which she pressed hard against Harper's wound.

"Oh my gosh, there's so much blood!" Kelly's hands were shaking against Harper's arm. "Mom! Mom! Help!"

Harper wanted to tell her sister not to worry, but she was feeling woozy. Her tongue felt swollen and heavy in her mouth. She looked toward the door and saw Michael standing in shock, a look of fear on his face. All of a sudden, she saw another boy flickering over him, like an old faded photograph. The boy was taller, with dark hair and sickly pale skin. She couldn't make out his face at all, except for his very dark eyes. His clothes were old-fashioned, like he belonged in a black-and-white movie. He wore a black sweater vest over a white collared shirt and long shorts that cinched below the knee. What kid wore a sweater vest? Her vision blurred and she blinked. The boy was gone.

"What happened?"

Harper could hear the panic in her mother's voice. Heard her yelling at Kelly to call 911.

She looked back at Michael but this time, instead of the flickering boy, she saw Michael's eyes change into dark, hollow unblinking eyes. They sent a cold rush through her body and an urgent desire to protect her brother. Who was this strange boy? Why was she seeing him? How had the fire truck moved? Did she really feel hands on her legs? So many questions. But the most important one of all she couldn't believe.

Was Dayo right? Was her house really haunted?

The last thing she remembered was hearing her mother say, "It's starting all over again."

And then she blacked out.

HARPER'S STUPID DC JOURNAL

Entry #6

Things I hate:

1. *Doctors*
2. *Hospitals*
3. *Emergency rooms*
4. *Pain*
5. *Stitches*
6. *Needles*
7. *Sick people*
8. *Blood*
9. *Antiseptic smell*
10. *Hospital gowns*
11. *Myself*

THE UNBELIEVER

Day 4–Thursday evening

She woke up in the emergency room, her mother holding her hand tightly while her father sat next to the bed. Her left arm was throbbing and her head hurt.

"I'm thirsty," she said.

Her father poured out a glass of ice water from the plastic pitcher on the side table and helped her sit up.

"It appears that falling down the stairs wasn't good enough, so you decided to give us a real scare this time, huh?" Peter joked. He caressed her hair as she finished the water.

"Don't kid around," Yuna reproved. "I nearly had

a heart attack today. There was so much blood."

"Twenty-five stitches later and you're good as new!" Peter said.

Yuna glared at her husband.

"It's over, honey, she's gonna be fine," he said, giving his wife a kiss. "They even said we could take her home once she woke up."

"But should she?" Yuna asked.

"What do you mean?" Harper was alarmed.

"I'm just not sure you are out of the woods yet," her mom said.

"No, you can't do that!" Harper exclaimed, her anger building. She could hear the hysterical note in her voice but she couldn't control it. "I can't stay here, please Dad, you can't leave me. Please let me go home. I want to go home!" Her heart was pounding in her throat as she tried to control her breathing. Her hands shook uncontrollably. She fought the tears that threatened to burst from her. She hated hospitals. They couldn't do this to her again.

Her father hugged her tight. "Don't worry, sweetheart. You are definitely going home today."

At his words she began to calm down. She pressed a shaky hand to her belly and took deep breaths. Her parents shared a look and Yuna closed her eyes as if in pain. Harper was surprised to see her mother appear so sad and ashamed.

"About the accident. Do you remember what happened?" Peter asked.

Harper furrowed her brows as a vision of the creepy truck and the weird dark-eyed boy flashed through her mind. She shuddered. It was just a dream. There was no strange boy, and the fire truck had not been moving by itself. She'd just imagined all that. They weren't real.

She raised a hand up to her face to try to hide her trembling lips.

"I was walking out of Michael's room and I must have tripped and fell on this old fire truck," she said slowly. "It was sharp and its ladder was sticking up. I think that was what cut me."

"I didn't see it in the room," her mother said. "When the ambulance came, they kept asking me how you'd hurt yourself, but we couldn't find anything."

Harper could feel the panic rising again at her mother's words. "It was there! I'm telling you it was an old antique-looking fire truck. It was all metal, and the edges were really sharp. That's how I got cut up."

"Hush," her father said, gathering her up in his arms. "Maybe it got pushed under the bed when you fell. We'll look for it when we get home. But in either case, you're going to have to get a tetanus shot just to be safe."

He left to get the nurse, pulling the curtain shut behind him. Harper found herself alone with her mother, who kept staring at her with teary eyes.

"I know you've never really forgiven me for sending you to Briarly," she said. "If it's any consolation to you, sending you there is my deepest regret. But you know I didn't have a choice, right?"

Harper glared at her mother. "I don't know that."

Her mother shook her head. "No, sweetie! There was no choice. Because you started the fire—"

"What do you mean I started the fire?"

Her mother stopped short. "Because the administration thought you started the fire, they said you had no choice but to go to Briarly."

"You think I started the fire, too?"

Yuna paused and then said gently, "I'm sure it was an accident."

"You think I started it," Harper whispered. She could feel her stomach churn with anxiety.

"Honey, there was no one else there but you," her mother replied.

Harper looked away, unable to process the information. She couldn't remember the fire at all. But there was no way she would have started it. She knew that in her heart.

"Why didn't you tell me before?" Harper asked.

"Julie and all your doctors said not to. That it would be better to let you try to remember these things on your own."

"Then why are you telling me this now?"

"Because I have to ask you." Her mother paused.

"Ask me what?"

"Honey, did you hurt yourself on purpose?"

At first Harper couldn't believe her ears. Was her mother accusing her of slicing up her own arm intentionally? Anger surged through her.

"Why bother asking?" Harper replied bitterly. "You wouldn't believe me, anyway. I want Grandma Lee. She's the only one who never judges me. I want her."

Before her mother could respond, her father returned with a nurse carrying a little silver tray with a bottle of medicine and a needle. As the nurse administered the shot, Harper glanced at her mother. For once her tightly wound, perfectionist mom seemed lost and out of sorts. Harper leaned closer to her father. Inside, she was a roller-coaster ride of emotions. Her mother didn't trust her. Her mother didn't believe her. But then could Harper believe herself?

HARPER'S STUPID DC JOURNAL

Entry #7

Things I hate:

1. *Weird unexplainable things*
2. *When people don't believe me*
3. *Not remembering*

I dreamed of a fire at my old school and a little blond girl with eyes like a cat.

I'm in my old art class and she keeps nagging at me to play with her. In my dream I whisper, "Leave me alone, Maddie." I'm sitting at my desk with my head down, trying to ignore her, but she's pulling at my ponytail and poking me in the head.

"Why won't you ever play with me?"

Maddie is dangerous, I can feel it. Instead of responding, my dream self runs for the door. But before I can reach it, Maddie grabs me by my hair and drags me back into the middle of the room.

I'm screaming one moment, and in the next I can hear Maddie's voice directly in my head. She keeps chanting over and over, Fire fire fire . . .

Somehow she's gotten hold of a butane torch that Mr. Manning keeps locked in the supply closet and she's heading straight for the windows where the papier-mâché projects had been set out to dry. I watch in horror as she pushes the button to ignite the torch and then turns the knob to get a huge flame. She's laughing as she holds the flame to the first project, a papier-mâché horse.

I'm yelling at her to stop but she won't listen, and as hard as I try, I can't move from where I'm standing. My legs won't work. And the fire spreads so fast. All the projects in the front window are ablaze and I can hear the fire alarms ringing. My head is hurting so much that it feels like someone is trying to hammer my brain into mush. Someone is screaming. I realize it is me. And then I wake up.

Was this fact or fiction?

I really hope it's true because then I'll know that I didn't set that fire.

HEALING WOUNDS

Day 5–Friday morning

Harper didn't wake up until late the next morning. She was groggy from the painkillers that the hospital had given her, and her arm and neck were still throbbing. Bad dreams had kept her from sleeping soundly.

Her father came in to check on her. He brought a breakfast tray with a bowl of hot oatmeal mixed with honey and berries.

"How's my girl?" he asked as he placed the tray on her lap.

"Not hungry," she said, trying to wave away the food. She groaned as she felt the sharp twinge of her stitches. "Everything hurts."

Her father shook his head and picked up a spoonful of oatmeal. "Eat anyway." He force-fed her the oatmeal. At the first taste of the sweet, warm dish, Harper suddenly felt ravenous. Taking the spoon from him, she began to eat.

"Where's Michael?" she asked. She kept thinking of her brother's shocked and fearful expression.

"Your mom dragged him and Kelly out to the store," he said. "I'm surprised you slept through it. He made a huge fuss."

"Why?"

"He didn't want to go. Said he needed to stay in his room," her father said with a puzzled look. "It's strange how the boy who was always running around outside suddenly turns into a homebody. I guess that's what happens when you move away and don't have any friends."

"Poor Michael," Harper said. "He hasn't been himself lately."

"Well, we're going to fix all that," her father said. "Michael is going to start swimming camp in two weeks, you'll start taking classes at the art center, and Kelly will take an SAT course."

"I thought that was online?"

"Well, we signed her up for a new class as a way for her to meet some of the kids in the area. It'll be good for all of you to make friends before the school year starts."

Harper was relieved to hear that Michael would go to summer camp and wouldn't be shut up in his room all day.

"Dad, when can we see Grandma Lee?"

"Believe it or not, your mom has been talking to your grandmother about coming over," he said. "She just wants the house completely ready beforehand. You know how Mom is. She wants everything perfect."

"That's why I'm such a disappointment," Harper whispered.

"Don't say that!" Peter said firmly. "You could never disappoint us."

Harper stayed quiet, but she knew the truth. She could never be the perfect child for her mother. How could she? Her mother even believed that she'd started the fire at her school.

Peter lifted Harper's arm and peeked under a corner of the bandage. Then he opened up a tube of medicine to smooth over Harper's neck wounds.

Harper winced. Everything throbbed in pain.

"Dad," Harper asked. "Do you think I started that fire at school?"

He froze midstand and sank back onto Harper's bed.

"Mom told me about the argument you guys had yesterday," he said.

"Well, do you?"

"No, honey. I don't," he said. "I don't know for sure what happened. But when you woke up at the hospital, you insisted that you didn't start the fire. And I have never doubted you."

Harper let out a long shaky breath. "Then why does Mom?"

"She doesn't doubt you, either, honey. She was so scared about your accident that she spoke without thinking."

Harper opened her mouth to refute it but stopped when she saw the pleading expression on her father's face. She sighed. She knew what he wanted. He didn't want her to argue with him about her mother. Her dad had a blind spot when it came to her mom. Even when she was completely wrong, he would make excuses for her. Harper didn't want to hear lies. She could believe her mother was scared by her accident. But the fear had brought out her mom's true feelings. What she really believed.

"I know I didn't start the fire," Harper said. "But

I don't remember what happened."

An image of the blond girl from her dream flashed through her head. She was a little fuzzy on her physical form, but the face was crystal clear. This could not be her imagination. This had to be a memory. She had to tell her dad.

Taking a deep breath, she looked up at her father's sympathetic face and the words froze in her throat. Suddenly, she was no longer so sure. Who was Maddie? Why did she start the fire? Or was the dream actually made up after all?

"I'm tired," Harper said. "I'm going to take a nap."

Day 5—Friday afternoon

A couple of hours later, as Harper lounged in bed, she heard the others return home.

Her mom and Kelly came in with a shopping bag.

"How are you feeling, honey?" Yuna asked. She sat and caressed Harper's face before checking her injuries.

"Okay," Harper said abruptly. She was still upset with her mother.

Then she gasped in delight when her mother put a giant box of chocolate almond Pepero sticks on her bed. They were her favorite cookies but were only available at Korean grocery stores. Her mom was really good at peace offerings.

"How'd you get them?"

Yuna smiled. "I found a Korean deli nearby that had them. I bought out their supply so you'll be all set for a while."

She sat holding Harper's hand for a long time before leaning over to whisper softly in her ear, "I love you, honey. Always. Please don't ever doubt that."

Yuna gave Harper a kiss and stood up. "Don't eat all of them today, though, okay?"

Kelly plopped her shopping bag on Harper's bed as their mom left the room.

"Mom wanted to get some stuff that you might like so I remembered the Nerdy Boy series you love so much. I picked up the latest book, and a how-to-draw-manga book and a new box of markers."

She handed the shopping bag to Harper, who dumped everything onto her lap.

"Oh man, this is awesome! Thanks, Kelly!" At the bottom of the bag, there was a little stuffed toy. It was a doughnut with a cute face and arms and legs. Harper laughed as she held it up for Kelly to see.

"Yeah, I thought of you as soon as I saw it," Kelly said with a smile. "Remember when you used to tell everyone that you wanted to be a doughnut when you grew up because you could eat a little of yourself whenever you were hungry?"

"You called me a doughnut cannibal and told me I would taste terrible," Harper said.

"Well, yeah, a human-flavored doughnut has got to be pretty awful."

Kelly laughed, and for a moment Harper remembered the good times she used to have with Kelly before she became a snotty high school teenager.

Kelly reached over and tugged lightly at Harper's hair. "Feel better, doughnut cannibal. I'm gonna go study."

A little while later, Michael crept into her room.

"Harper, are you all right?" he asked in a tiny voice.

She sat up, ignoring the sharp pain, and opened her arms wide. Michael ran into them, hugging her tight.

"What's the matter, little buddy?" she asked.

"I don't know if I like Billy anymore," Michael whispered. "I don't think he's a good friend."

"Why? What's he doing?"

"He always wants to show me things, but I don't

like it. I tell him to stop but he never listens to me. It gives me a headache."

"What does he show you?"

"Things," he said vaguely. "But I want him to stop."

"Then you need to tell him to go away," Harper said.

Her little brother shook his head. "He doesn't listen to me! He says he's older and he's in charge. And I think he hurt you. It was his fire truck that made you fall."

Harper gasped. "I knew I didn't imagine it. But where is the fire truck?"

"I put it in the attic," he said. "I don't even want to look at it anymore. He made me mad when he hurt you."

The attic. The place Billy warned them not to go.

"I don't get it. Why would he want to hurt me?" Harper asked.

"Because he doesn't like you," Michael said. "He thinks you are going to stop us from being friends. But I don't want to be friends with him. He's a bully and a bad boy! I don't want him to live with us in our house anymore."

At his words, Harper had the jolt of another vision. She was yelling at someone, but she couldn't see who it was. All she could hear was her own voice shouting: *Go away! Leave me alone!*

"Harper, are you listening to me?"

She shook her head hard. She needed to focus on her brother's problems.

"I'm sorry, Michael, what did you say?"

"You have to tell Billy to go away."

Harper paused and took a deep breath.

"Michael, Billy is not real."

Michael looked at Harper in shock. "He is so. How do you think you got hurt? He hurt you!"

Harper shook her head, trying to block out the memory of the moving fire truck and the feeling of hands on her legs.

"It was an accident. Billy's your imaginary friend. He might look and seem real to you, but he's not. You have the power. You can tell him to go away forever, and he has to listen."

Michael looked at her doubtfully. "He doesn't listen to me, Harper."

Play with me, Harper! Or I'll make you!

She shuddered and closed her eyes, trying to block out the voice.

"Michael, you need to be strong," she said. "You are the boss. You are in charge. Block him. Ignore him. Eventually, he will go away."

Harper spoke as much for herself as she did for Michael.

Michael nodded, but his solemn expression showed disbelief.

"Harper, can I stay in your room tonight?"

She smiled in delight. "I'd love that."

HARPER'S STUPID DC JOURNAL

Entry #8

Things I hate:

1. There are no corner pizzerias or delis anywhere near me.

2. My headaches

This house makes my head hurt. I had the worst headache today after a really strange memory. At least I think it was a memory. I was watching TV and there was a girl on the screen with bright-red hair. It reminded me of a friend I used to have.

I'm in my room, hiding under a blanket fort and whispering secrets with my best friend. I can see her bouncy red curls but her face is a dark circle, as if the light was too bright behind her.

The harder I try to see her face, the more my head starts to hurt.

But no matter how hard I try, I can't see her face.

I don't know if it's fact or fiction.

THE ATTIC

Day 6—Saturday morning

Saturday was another scorching Washington, D.C., morning. Harper was restless and uneasy.

When Dayo stopped by, Harper was relieved to the point of tears. Dayo came alone, without Pumpkin, but with a big container of her mother's oatmeal, white chocolate, and cranberry cookies. Harper's mom brought up a tray with large ice-cold glasses of milk to enjoy with their snack, as well as a bowl of popcorn.

"How are you feeling?" Dayo asked.

"I'm all right," Harper replied. "Sick of being in this room, though."

"How many stitches did you get?"

“Twenty-five,” Harper said as she peeled back the gauze pads to show her friend.

“You know, that’s the second serious injury you’ve gotten since moving in,” Dayo said. She was sitting on the bottom of the bed, her knees drawn up to her chin. “And you haven’t even been here that long.”

Harper sighed. She knew where Dayo was headed.

“I know you don’t believe in ghosts and stuff, but you have to be careful!” Dayo pulled several pieces of folded paper out of her pocket. “I did some research and found out some really interesting things about the history of this house. It was built in 1889 by Professor Alfred Mitchell Grady, who was a chemist fascinated with the afterlife. He believed in spiritualism, which I think is just the belief in ghosts and stuff. His wife died in childbirth right when they moved into the house and afterward, Professor Grady spent much of his time with a famous medium named Eudora Dubois. I had to look up what a medium is, but it’s like a psychic who can talk to the dead. Anyway, Professor Grady thought that if he could learn about the afterlife from the dead, then he could gain the secret to immortality. So he had Ms. Dubois hold a lot of séances and apparently he did some weird, bad experiments on homeless people.”

“Experiments? What kind?” Harper asked.

"Didn't say what they were, but they were bad enough that the police began investigating him. When the police came to the house to arrest him, they found Ms. Dubois dead at her séance table and no sign of Professor Grady. That was in 1913. Rumor has it that he made a pact with the Devil and is living an immortal life somewhere."

Harper shuddered. Ever since she was little, she'd always been frightened of the Devil. "Not allowed to say the D-word here. Too scary."

"Sorry," Dayo said absentmindedly as she continued to read. "In 1925, the Bellair family moved in and suffered a terrible tragedy when their oldest son, William, died in an accident that same year. He was eight at the time."

"Oh, that's sad," Harper said. "What happened?"

"It doesn't say in this article. But afterward the house passed to the Richmonds, who lived here a long time. Their only daughter sold it to the Jacobs family in 1965."

"Hey, if the Richmonds lived here for so long, why isn't it called the Richmond house instead?"

"Probably because nothing happened to them," Dayo said.

"For forty years?" Harper asked.

"Yeah, nothing that was newsworthy, anyway. But

the Jacobs had a son who got really sick and almost died. He went to the hospital and was on the mend, but as soon as he came home, he got worse again. So he went back to the hospital and his family moved out of the house for good. After the Jacobs moved out, it changed ownership five times. None of them stayed long until the last family, the McCarthys, moved in. The mom was arrested for abuse and attempted murder of her six-year-old son. The son survived and was sent to live with his grandparents. Mrs. McCarthy pleaded not guilty by reason of insanity because she claimed that her son had been possessed by an evil spirit and she was only trying to save him."

The image of the evil boy flashed through Harper's mind. "That's awful."

"What's awful is that you've had two freak accidents in a row. Something in this house doesn't like you," Dayo said.

"There's probably nothing here," Harper said practically. "I guess I'm just really, really klutzy."

Her friend looked doubtful.

"I think you want my house to be haunted because you think it would be cool," Harper teased.

Dayo's eyes went wide. "Well, I mean haunted houses are cool, but I wouldn't want to live in one.

No offense, Harper. But I can't even imagine what it would be like to have a ghost hanging around all the time."

Harper pulled a small throw blanket from her bed and covered her head with it.

"I am the ghost of the old Grady house and I'm here to steal your soul, ooooooh."

A pillow crashed into her head and Harper threw off the blanket with a laugh.

"It's not funny," Dayo said. "What if there really is a ghost or a spirit in this house that is out to get you like it did in the past? Aren't you scared?"

"Well, in those stories it was only boys that got hurt, right? So I should be safe."

"What about Michael?"

Harper suddenly flashed back to her brother's words.

You have to tell Billy to go away.

"Earth to Harper, come in Harper," Dayo was repeating over and over.

"Sorry," Harper said. "I was just spacing out."

"You had the weirdest look on your face," Dayo said. "Like you were constipated or something."

Harper sputtered indignantly. "I did not!"

"Yes, you looked like this." Dayo scrunched up

her face, making Harper laugh.

"Oh, so my thinking face looks like I'm constipated?"

"Well, I don't know what you were thinking about, but it sure wasn't happy."

Of course it wasn't. But what could she possibly tell Dayo without her new friend thinking she was crazy? While Dayo was the one who was always bringing up ghosts, it would be an entirely different thing to tell her that she was beginning to think a ghost was bothering her brother. That sounded too strange, even to her!

She thought about the old fire truck that had hurt her. Michael had said it was Billy's. He said he'd put it in the attic. It was the one part of the house her parents hadn't touched yet. There were still piles of old things up there left behind from previous owners. Harper kept thinking about that fire truck. She needed to find it and get rid of it. Maybe then Michael would return to normal.

"I was thinking about the attic," Harper said. "My dad told me it's filled with tons of junk from the old owners. My mom won't let him throw anything away just in case there's a valuable antique up there, but if the house is really haunted, I bet the stuff up there might be haunted, too."

Curiosity gleamed in Dayo's eyes, mixed with a healthy dose of fear. Harper could see that her friend was interested in the prospect of ghost hunting.

"I'm gonna go up and take a look, you want to come with me?"

Dayo looked at Harper's injuries doubtfully. "Aren't you supposed to stay in bed?"

"What's the matter, you chicken?" Harper scoffed. She got up gingerly from her bed, trying not to grimace in pain. She shot Dayo a thumbs-up and opened the door. They both stepped into the hallway and looked at each other nervously.

"You sure you're up for this?" Harper asked.

Dayo nodded, apprehension and excitement bubbling in her eyes. "Let's go!"

They walked down to the other end of the hallway, past the bathroom, and stopped at the hall closet to grab two flashlights. At the very far corner, there was a narrow door with a latch to keep it closed. Harper wondered how Michael had reached the latch when she noticed a footstool nearby. She pulled open the door with a loud creak and turned on the light. The stairway was dim, narrow, and smelled of musty old things. The stairs creaked with every step and Dayo giggled as she held tight to the back of Harper's shirt.

"It sure does sound like a haunted house," she said.

Even with sunlight pouring in from a few windows, the attic was mostly dark corners and musty coverings. The girls turned on their flashlights to peer into the corners and avoid the loose objects scattered all over the floor. There were old bookshelves filled with boxes and knickknacks so dust covered that Harper couldn't even guess what they were.

"Wow, this looks like it could be hundreds of years old," Dayo said as she peered through a box of yellowed papers.

"Probably just a hundred," Harper said. "But that's still old."

As she shone her light into the corners, she stopped short as she caught a reflective gleam. She'd found the fire truck. It was the only item in the entire attic that wasn't covered in dust.

"That's it," she said. She walked over to the bookcase and picked up the truck. "This was what I cut myself on. Michael said he put it back up here after my accident."

Dayo held her light over the fire truck but refused to touch it.

"It's so old and gross," she said. "And it's got blood all over it."

"That would be mine," Harper said. Blood had dried over the white ladder, leaving it dark and dirty.

Dayo took a step back. "I don't like it," she said. "It gives me the creeps. You should get rid of it."

She shone the flashlight in the far corner.

"Oh, wow, look at this!"

Harper turned to see Dayo pointing to the other side of the attic where there was a long table and an old-fashioned armoire. This part of the attic was not as cluttered or dusty. It looked as if someone had attempted to keep it clean. Harper peered fascinated through the glass widows of the armoire. All sorts of instruments could be seen hanging inside. Violins, triangles, flutes, small guitars, cymbals, and so many other things. She turned the knob but couldn't open it.

"It's locked," Harper mused out loud. "I wonder where the key is?"

"I bet it's somewhere in one of these little boxes," Dayo replied.

The table next to it was covered by an old yellowed blanket. Dayo had lifted up the blanket to expose a desk filled with many strange and exotic things. On one corner, there was a series of large and small wooden boxes, some plain and some ornately decorated. Harper opened a black lacquered box with colorful flowers painted on the lid. A small ballerina popped up and began to twirl to a sweet music-box tune. It only went around once before it began to slow down.

The other corner had six conelike instruments in silver and wood. On the side of one of the biggest cones were the words "Spirit Trumpet" etched along its length. Next to them were several wooden tablets of various sizes, the largest of which had a sign that read, "What does Planchette say? Jacques & Son, London."

Harper picked it up to take a closer look. "I wonder what this is."

"I think it goes with that," Dayo said, pointing at an ancient-looking board with numbers and letters. Weird-looking cards with strange imagery lay all around it.

"What is all this?"

"I know," Dayo said in hushed tones. "That's a Ouija board and tarot cards. And look!" She lifted the cover to expose the rest of the table. "A crystal ball!"

"Cool!" Harper moved forward to touch the shining globe when Dayo shook her head quickly and covered it again.

"We shouldn't touch any of these things," Dayo said. "My mom says things like that bring bad spirits to you, so it's best not to ever touch them."

Nodding, Harper backed away. She had no intention of attracting any more bad things. She looked down and realized she was still holding the planchette thing. She dropped it on the table and jumped in horror when it began to spin all by itself. The atmosphere in the attic suddenly felt heavy and expectant.

"No, Harper! You put it on the Ouija board! You have to move it, quickly!"

Harper didn't want to touch it, but she forced herself to grab the spinning thing and throw it on the other side of the table.

Dayo shuddered. "Let's get out of here!"

They were heading back toward the stairs when there was a loud crash, making them jump. Harper shone her light in front of them and noticed a tower of boxes had fallen in their path. Hundreds of shiny colorful marbles rolled everywhere and tinny-sounding music came from behind the boxes surrounding them. Harper felt the hair on the back of her neck stand up as the sounds of the rolling marbles and the tinny music mixed with the creaking of the attic floor. An oppressive feeling surrounded her. She started to move, but Dayo gripped her arm tightly, causing Harper to grimace in pain.

"Sorry," Dayo whispered. "I'm scared." Letting go, she grabbed the back of Harper's shirt instead.

They walked forward, Harper still clutching the fire truck in her arms with Dayo close behind her. The scratchy music kept repeating itself. They rounded an old coffee table piled high with boxes and papers and found a mess before them. Several more boxes had fallen down, spilling out books and knickknacks wrapped in old yellowed newspaper. The sound was coming from underneath a pile of old clothes. Harper pushed the clothing to the side with her foot and uncovered a small, dirty yellow box with a crank.

"It's one of those old jack-in-the-boxes," Dayo said. "The fall must have triggered it, so that it started playing."

"Wow, you sure do know a lot!" Harper said, admiring.

Dayo smiled. "I watch a lot of *Antiques Roadshow* when I'm helping my mom with her baking."

Harper picked up the jack-in-the-box and turned it over. "How do you get it to stop?"

She grabbed the lever and gave it a turn but

nothing happened. The tinny music kept playing. Dayo let go of Harper's shirt and took hold of the jack-in-the-box.

"It must be stuck," she said. She cranked the lever hard and then shook it. "Hmmmm, I guess it must be broken."

They stood close together examining the box. Suddenly the lid flew open and a frightful-looking clown sprang out of the opening, its big red hands waving madly while its scary face bobbled before the girls' faces.

Harper and Dayo screamed and tripped over the marbles, sending them both flailing to the ground. The jack-in-the-box fell on the floor before them, the maniacal clown bouncing forward as if it was trying to break free of its restraints.

Scrambling to their feet, the girls raced down the stairs and out onto the second-floor landing. Harper slammed the attic door and latched it. Her heart was hammering in her chest. Every muscle in her body was aching and she could feel the tight pull of the stitches from her injury. Dayo kept running toward Harper's room, and Harper ran after her and dove for her bed. Dayo climbed in next to her as they huddled close together. They looked at each other silently before bursting into laughter.

"Your face was so funny!" Dayo said in between her giggles.

"Yours, too," Harper wheezed. "You looked like you saw a ghost."

"That stupid jack-in-the-box," Dayo exclaimed. "Seriously, that clown was so freaky. It nearly gave me a heart attack."

Harper wiped the tears from her eyes as she nodded in agreement. "No lie, I nearly wet my pants."

Dayo threw herself back, still giggling. "Gah! I really thought it was a ghost for a second there."

Before she could answer, Harper realized she no longer held the fire truck.

"Oh dang it, I must have dropped the fire truck."

Dayo looked up at the ceiling, her eyes wide as she shook her head. "No way! I'm never going up there again."

"Me neither."

They both laughed even harder.

When they finally calmed down, Dayo said, "Hey, tomorrow is Sunday and we always go to ten a.m. mass at Our Lady of Mercy. You should come with us. I'll even bring a flask so we can get you some holy water."

Harper looked at her friend doubtfully. "But I

told you I'm not Catholic."

Dayo waved her hands, unconcerned. "That's okay. I just want to get you some holy water, anyway. To keep you safe."

Harper still wasn't sure. "I don't know."

"Well, think about it. I know I'll feel better once you have something to protect you," she said. She gave Harper a hug, mindful of her wound. "Be careful."

HARPER'S STUPID DC JOURNAL

Entry #9

Things I hate:

1. *Dust*
2. *Old decaying things*
3. *Clowns*

I really hated that jack-in-the-box clown. I can't believe people bought those things as toys for little kids. That's just so wrong. I've never understood why grown-ups hire clowns for little kids' birthday parties. Clowns are scary. I have one clear memory from when I was five years old, at a Halloween party. I was picking out some candy from a big bowl when I realized someone was behind me. When I turned around I was face-to-face with a big, creepy, smiling clown. I cried so hard. It was Grandma Lee who comforted me and showed me that the clown was a person with heavy makeup on and an ugly wig. But still, I've never gotten over my fear of them.

Something about the clown in the attic made me as scared as I was that day. It made me feel as if the house is alive and trying to frighten me, trying to get rid of me.

What with all the weird stuff we found in the attic and the research Dayo is doing online, I feel that trying to understand why this house is so creepy means having to find out about the previous owners. The weird thing is that when I googled my home address, I found this entire website dedicated to old Mr. Grady, the first owner of the house. Apparently, Dayo was right. He was a serious weirdo. He believed that if he could harness the power of the spirit world, then he could find the secret to immortality. That's why he conducted experiments on poor people who had no families of their own. He would invite them for a home-cooked meal made by Eudora Dubois. The website says she was a fake medium with no real powers and was just Grady's accomplice. Ms. Dubois would poison the food with strychnine, which was used back then as rat poison.

Fact—Even a little bit of strychnine is enough to kill a grown man and Ms. Dubois put enough poison in the food to cause immediate seizures and death within the hour. While the victims convulsed, Grady would use electric shock on them and record his findings. It was the worst kind of torture.

So, this house really had a lot of death in it. That explains why it is so creepy. But I can't help but wonder . . . what ever happened to Grady? They say his body was never found. Does that mean he's still in the house somewhere? Maybe he's haunting the house and I have to find his rotting bones to get rid of him.

Ugh. I might never be able to fall asleep again.

THE TRANSFORMATION

Day 6—Saturday afternoon

Harper called to Michael, but he wasn't answering again. She knocked on his door. After a long moment, she heard him shout, "Go away!" but she opened the door anyway. She noticed the new area rug in the middle of the room, replacing the one she had bled on. Michael stood near the window. In his hands, he held the antique fire truck.

"I thought you said you put the truck in the attic," she said.

Michael didn't turn around. "It's mine," he said. "I like it." His voice was flat and emotionless.

Harper walked in front of Michael and stared down into his face. He looked like a zombie. When she went to touch him, he growled at her, his face taking on the fierce expression of a wild baboon. “Don’t touch me!”

“Michael,” Harper asked, “why are you acting this way?”

“I just want you to go away,” he said. “If you don’t, you’ll be sorry.”

Harper was alarmed. Michael had never threatened her before! She needed to get him out of his room, away from whatever it was that was holding him captive.

“Come on, little buddy.” She wrapped an arm around his shoulders and tried to turn him toward the door. “Let’s go get some ice cream.”

Michael spun away quickly and raised the truck up as if to strike her with it. Harper backed off immediately.

“Hey, are you okay?” she asked.

He didn’t answer, staring back at her with a blank look in his eyes. Harper felt a sharp sense of unease and she thought back to their recent conversation. *You have to tell Billy to go away.*

“Michael, is Billy still bothering you?”

The effect was immediate. His face contorted with rage.

“Leave me alone! Or I’ll sock you right in the beezer.”

His voice had no expression whatsoever, making it all the more frightening. Alarm had slipped away and was replaced by a deepening dread that filled the pit of Harper's stomach. Michael would never threaten anyone with violence. It was not in his nature.

"What are you talking about? What's a beezer?" she asked.

"Your big fat ugly nose," he said. "Now get out!"

Harper remained where she was, too stunned to move. She couldn't help but think that this was not her brother.

"I said get out, ya big boob!" He threw the truck at Harper, narrowly missing her.

"What's going on in here?" Harper's mom stood at the doorway, peering in, her eyebrows furrowed in concern.

Michael's face changed from rage to adoration.

"Mommy!" he yelled. He raced over and wrapped his arms around her waist. "You came back for me!"

"Honey, I've been here all day," she replied, patting his head. "Harper, how are you feeling?"

Before Harper could reply, Michael cut in. "Don't talk to her, she's being really mean to me and I hate her," he said. "She said she wished I was dead!"

Both Harper and her mom gasped.

"Harper, how could you say something like that?"

"I never said that. He's lying! And he tried to hit me with his fire truck. You know, the same thing that cut me and gave me twenty-five stitches!"

She leaned down to pick it up off the ground, but Michael beat her to it. Yuna looked sharply at the toy that Michael now held tightly in his arms.

"Let me see that," she said.

Michael hid the truck behind him. "No, it's mine. She can't have it!"

"Michael, you need to give it to me now." Yuna's voice was calm but stern.

With a furious glare at Harper, Michael handed it to his mom. Yuna looked over the fire truck, staring carefully at the dried blood all over the once white ladder.

"This is what cut you so badly," Yuna stated matter-of-factly.

Harper nodded.

Yuna turned to Michael. "Did you hide this from me after the accident? Did you do that on purpose? You know I was looking for the thing that hurt your sister."

Michael burst into tears. "I didn't do nothing! She's just trying to get me in trouble!"

Yuna dropped to her knees and gathered him up

in her arms. "Oh honey, I'm sure there's a misunderstanding here."

Wrapped in his mother's arms, Michael's face looked happy, like his normal self. Harper started to wonder if she had imagined it all . . . that is, until he opened his eyes.

Harper nearly fell back in shock. His eyes were so dark, so hollow, so dead.

This was not her brother.

And then he blinked, and his eyes were normal again.

There was a knocking on the door and Kelly popped her head in. "Mom, I thought we were going shopping now."

"Yes, of course," Yuna said. She put Michael down and took the fire truck again. "You can't have this truck for now. I'll give it back to you tomorrow."

But Michael's attention had strayed from the truck. "Where are you going?"

"I'm taking your sister shopping and will be back by dinner," Yuna replied.

"I don't want you to go with her," Michael said. "I want you to stay with me."

"It's okay, sweetheart," Yuna said, caressing his hair. "We'll be back soon."

"Don't be a brat," Kelly said as she and Yuna

headed for the stairs.

Harper followed Michael into the hallway and took notice of how intensely he was staring at Kelly. He was so focused, he paid no attention to Harper. But Harper took close notice of the cold anger that emanated from him. His little face was distorted with a feral scowl that stunned Harper.

When the front door slammed shut behind them, Michael walked past Harper and into his room. Only when he closed the door did Harper feel free to leave.

HARPER'S STUPID DC JOURNAL

Entry #10

Things I hate:

1. *Hearing strange things in the house*
2. *Hearing strange things in my head*
3. *Weird dreams*

I'm in a room that looks sort of like my living room but completely different. The furniture's all wood stuff and the sofa has a weird grandmotherly pattern. In the corner, there's an ancient record player, I think they used to call them phonographs. I remember seeing them in old black-and-white movies.

I think this might be my house because it has big french windows like the ones my mom raved about when we moved in. And outside, the same huge magnolia tree stands right in front of them. It also leads out into the foyer area that looks just like ours. I think I'm dreaming of my house from a long time ago. But I have no idea why.

Suddenly, a little boy runs into the room holding several toy cars. He's being chased by an angry-looking older boy. There's something familiar about the older one. But I don't know what.

The little boy looks like he's Michael's age. He sits down on the carpet in the middle of the floor and begins playing with his cars. The older boy just stands there staring at him with the meanest expression on his face, like he really hates him. He walks over and snatches one of the cars out of the little boy's hand.

"No fair, William, that's mine! Give it back!"

William turns away and starts slamming the little car on the floor, sending a few of its wheels flying.

"Stop it! You're breaking it!"

"Shut up, Jonathan, or I'll give you what for!"

Jonathan tries to grab the car back, but William shoves him violently to the ground.

"I'm gonna tell Mommy!"

I catch an angry expression on William's face, and it gives me a bad feeling. I want to yell at Jonathan, tell him to run away. But all I can do is gasp in horror as William smashes the toy car into Jonathan's face, causing his nose to gush blood. He starts screaming, and a woman who must be their mother runs in.

"Oh my goodness! Jonathan!" The woman kneels by the screaming boy and pulls him into her lap. She takes out a large, flowy handkerchief from her apron pocket and holds it to Jonathan's nose.

"Did you hit Jonathan again?" she asks William in a harsh voice.

William starts shaking his head and denying it. The strangest part is the change in him when he sees his mother.

He looks at her with adoring and pleading eyes, even as he lies to her face.

The woman eyes William suspiciously and then turns back to Jonathan.

"Tell me what happened," she says.

The little boy is sobbing so hard he can't respond.

"Calm down, Jonathan, and tell me what happened. Did your brother do this?"

The love that shines in William's eyes as he looks at his mother vanishes immediately. He glares at his brother over her shoulder. I see him shake his head slowly as he catches Jonathan's frightened gaze.

"No, Mommy," Jonathan says. "I fell down."

I can't blame Jonathan for lying. His brother is really scary.

The mother whirls around to stare at William. It sickens me to see how quickly he changes back into an adoring boy again.

After a long moment, she sighs and stands up with Jonathan in her arms.

"Let's go put something cold on that." She hugs him tight and walks out of the room.

William watches them leave with such an intense expression of jealousy and hatred that I start to feel sorry for him. But then he spots Jonathan's cars on the ground and stomps on them with his heavy hard-soled shoes, mangling them until they're nothing but a pile of broken-up pieces. Then the strangest thing happens—he looks up and stares straight into my eyes. As if he can see me. His smile is so creepy that I wake up with a jolt.

I don't understand why I'm having such a weird dream. Who is this kid? And why is he so creepy? His smile is evil. And there's something wrong with his eyes. They look old, real old.

Fact—I don't know this boy.

Fact—I'm scared of him.

THE ACCIDENT

Day 7–Sunday afternoon

After lunch, Dayo came over with Pumpkin again to entertain Harper. This time Mrs. Clayton sent chocolate fudge cookies that were so divine Harper inhaled three before her mother could even pour her a glass of milk.

"Your mom is the best baker in the whole world," Harper said.

Her friend nodded as she dipped her cookie in her milk. "Our church always begs her for baked goods for our bake sales, because they know her stuff sells out."

"Well, if your mother ever decides to open up her own bakery, we will be her best customers," Harper's mother said. She stood next to Harper and began examining her stitches.

"How're you feeling?" Dayo asked.

"They still hurt a little," Harper said.

"When do you get the stitches out?"

Harper shrugged and looked at her mother.

Yuna smiled. "Just a few more days and we can get them removed."

Just then, Michael wandered into the kitchen, a strange, vacant expression on his face.

"Hi honey, you want a cookie? Dayo's mom made them, and they are out of this world," Yuna said. She offered the plate to Michael. At first he shook his head and turned away. But then his eyes locked on Pumpkin, who was sitting on Dayo's lap. Still staring at the dog, he reached over and took a cookie before walking out again.

"What's with your brother?" Dayo asked.

Harper shrugged. How could she say what she really thought? That her brother was acting like an entirely different person? One she really didn't like. That she thought it might be the ghost of a child who had lived in the house long ago?

Harper turned a troubled gaze toward her mother. How could she not see that something was wrong with him? Did she not notice the difference?

"He's been really weird lately," Harper said finally.

"He's just a little out of sorts," her mother said. "I think it's a combination of the big move, a new house, and no friends yet. He'll start camp soon. Hopefully, that'll help."

Dayo nodded. "It must be hard for him not to have anybody to play with."

Harper didn't respond. Not having a friend was not the problem.

"Now, you girls let me know if you need anything else. I'll be in my office," her mother said.

Harper and Dayo moved to the living room to hang out and watch TV. When they saw Michael again, he was still holding the same cookie, uneaten. Harper caught him crumbing his cookie and letting it fall to the ground as he walked out into the foyer. Pumpkin jumped down and went to eat the crumbs, following the trail out of the room. Suspicious of her brother's actions, Harper decided to go after them when they heard a loud yelp and Pumpkin came limping back. She was holding her front right leg up and whimpering. Michael ran after her, causing the little dog to hide behind Dayo's legs, trembling in fear.

"What did you do?" Harper demanded.

"I didn't do nothing," Michael said. His voice was

belligerent and he stood with his hands in fists by his sides. It was such an odd pose for him. Harper was once again struck by how wrong he was acting.

"Then why is Pumpkin hurt?"

Michael shrugged. "I might have stepped on her."

Dayo scooped her up and was cradling her.

"She's shaking! I'd better take her to the vet," Dayo said. "I hope her leg's not broken."

"My mom will take us," Harper said.

She ran yelling for her mother, who popped out of her office. Upon hearing what had happened, she told Harper to go get her father in the den, while she went to check on Pumpkin. Harper shouted for his attention and then rushed him back to the living room where Dayo stood anxiously holding the whimpering dog. Yuna looked up with a serious expression on her face.

"I think it might be broken," she said. She shot a troubled look at Michael.

Peter took a close look and agreed. "I'll take him," he said.

He pulled on his shoes and grabbed the keys off the foyer table. "Young man, your mom and I are going to have a serious talk with you when I get home. I want to find out exactly what happened."

Michael glowered at their father. No remorse, no

guilt, only anger was clear on his face.

"In the meantime, I want you to apologize to Dayo and Pumpkin," Peter said.

Michael turned away and ran to Yuna, bursting into tears and hugging her legs.

"Mommy, they're yelling at me. Tell them to stop."

The little dog kept whining in pain.

Yuna shook her head helplessly and motioned for them to go. When Harper looked over at Michael, she was shocked to see a little smile playing on his lips.

"Let's get her to the animal hospital right away. You can call your mom in the car," Peter told Dayo.

He opened the door and ushered Dayo and Harper out. As they left, Harper could see Michael gazing adoringly at Yuna. But her mother looked troubled.

Several hours later, they dropped a newly casted Pumpkin and Dayo home to her waiting mother. Harper's father talked with Mrs. Clayton while Harper helped carry Pumpkin into the house. The usually energetic dog was quiet and exhausted from her ordeal. Pumpkin's right front leg was now set in a bright-blue cast. Dayo and Harper placed the little dog on her bed and sat down in front of her. Pumpkin scooted over and laid her head in Dayo's lap and placed her unbroken front paw on Harper's leg.

"I think she's trying to tell you not to feel so bad," Dayo said with a little laugh.

Harper caressed the dog's soft fur, trying to keep back her tears. "I'm sorry, Pumpkin," she said.

"It was really nice of your father to take care of the hospital bill," Dayo said. "I'm sure my grandmother will really appreciate that."

"But it was our fault! Pumpkin would never have gotten hurt if you hadn't brought her over to our house," Harper said. "I just don't understand how Michael could have done this to her."

Dayo frowned. "It had to be an accident. He couldn't possibly have meant to hurt her, right?"

Harper bit her lip hard. The churning in the pit of her stomach told her that it wasn't an accident. What was happening to her brother?

She heard her father calling her and got up to leave.

"I'll come visit tomorrow," Harper said.

She waved good-bye and left the house. Mrs. Clayton smiled her usual sweet smile as Harper left.

"Don't worry about Pumpkin, sweetheart," Mrs. Clayton said. "She'll be good as new real soon. You come over and visit anytime, okay? I'll bake you cookies."

Mrs. Clayton's kindness only made Harper feel worse. She smiled and thanked her as she got in her father's car. Suddenly Dayo shouted, "Wait a minute!"

She ran back into the house and reappeared a minute later, completely out of breath. Running to Harper, she handed her a small plastic flask filled with water.

"I got this at Our Lady of Mercy this morning. Fresh holy water to keep you safe, Harper!" Dayo hugged Harper tight through the open car window and then went back inside.

They drove the few blocks in silence, Harper clutching the holy water in her hands. When they parked in the driveway, her father held her back to question her.

"Do you think Michael hurt Pumpkin on purpose?" he asked.

Harper ran a hand through her hair, tugging at it a little in frustration. After a pause she nodded. It was hard to think her sweet little brother could be capable of such a thing.

Peter leaned back in his seat, looking defeated. "I don't know what has gotten into him lately. I didn't think the move would be that hard on him because he's younger and so good-natured. But it's like he's turned into an entirely different boy. Like someone replaced our sweet little Michael with one I don't even recognize anymore."

Listening to her father triggered her memory of the strange dark-eyed boy Harper saw in Michael's room when the fire truck attacked her. Just the thought of him sent a cold chill through her. But he wasn't real. He couldn't be. There was no such thing as ghosts.

A memory flashed through her mind again.

Harper, she's not real! Rose is not real!

She could hear Kelly's voice yelling at her.

"Rose," Harper whispered.

"What did you say?" her father asked.

Harper bit her lip in alarm and shook her head.

"Did you say 'Rose'?"

Harper didn't answer.

"Rose was the name of the imaginary friend you used to have," he said carefully. "You've haven't mentioned her since . . ." His voice faded away. Harper knew what he was going to say. *Ever since Briarly.*

"I had an imaginary friend," Harper mused out loud.

"Yes, Rose always brought you a lot of joy," he said. "But don't mention her to your mom. She never approved."

Of course not, Harper thought.

"What made you think of her?" her father asked.

Harper shrugged. "I don't know."

She looked at her father for a long minute, taking in his concerned expression. What could she tell him that would sound even a little believable? *Dad, I think Michael is being possessed by his imaginary friend, who might be an evil ghost?*

"Don't worry about me, Dad," Harper said with a small smile. "You need to deal with Michael right now. I'm worried about him." Opening the car door, she hurried out and ran toward the house, ignoring her father as he called after her.

HARPER'S STUPID DC JOURNAL

Entry #11

Things I hate:

1. Not knowing what's fact and what's fiction

2. Remembering Rose has made me remember something else. But it's so unbelievable, it can't be real.

I was four years old, sitting in the living room with my babysitter and Kelly. My babysitter was busy talking on her phone and Kelly was watching television. There was a bowl of grapes on the coffee table, but I didn't want them. I wanted chocolate. And I knew where it was, too. My mom always kept the yummy chocolate squares in the pretty bowl on the table near the front door.

I scooted on my butt until I reached the edge of the sofa. I peered over at Kelly and the babysitter, but neither of them was watching me. Grinning, I sneaked around the sofa and crawled into the hallway so they couldn't see me. A shipment of packages had been delivered earlier in the day. They weren't heavy so I pushed the boxes in front of the table. Then I carefully lifted one of the boxes on top of the other and began to climb. My perch was wobbly but when I reached the mirror, I lost all interest in the candy. For in the mirror above the candy bowl, there was a girl smiling at me. She had curly red hair and light-blue eyes against overly pale skin. She waved hello but didn't speak. I leaned forward to touch the girl in the mirror, but suddenly felt the box under my feet slip away. As I fell, I saw the girl in the mirror and her horrified face. But before I hit the hardwood floor, I was caught by what felt like a pillow of air. Like I was being carried by the wind. I was caught in the ghostly embrace of the red-haired girl.

"My name is Rose," the ghost girl said. "And you are Harper."

I was so excited I clapped my hands. "Are you my friend?"

Rose nodded solemnly.

"Always," she said. "But don't tell anyone. It's a secret."

Is this a memory, dream, or my imagination playing tricks on me? I don't know what to think. Is Rose real or imaginary? Or was she a ghost?

WILLIAM BELLAIR

Day 8–Early Monday morning

Harper stood in front of the foyer mirror staring intently into every corner, wondering if she would find someone else staring back. Fifteen minutes later, she conceded defeat and sat down on the bench.

"There's no such thing as ghosts," she sighed.

An odd glinting in the mirror caught her attention. She peered at it, wondering what it was. The slight shimmer across the mirror reminded Harper of how a heat wave would distort objects in the distance. Mesmerized, she kept watching the shifting movement, lulled into a trance until she felt herself pulled in, as if she were falling into the mirror.

Harper found herself in a dreamlike state. She was outside, staring at a very white, very new-looking version of her house. She could hear the voices of boys playing in the backyard. She moved toward the noise, where she found the two boys from her previous dream chasing a ball. The big boy, William, would snatch the ball from the younger one, Jonathan, and then kick it far away. Jonathan kept chasing the ball until they finally reached a section of the backyard that was fenced off with chicken wire. William pulled the wire aside and walked over to what appeared to be an abandoned well, boarded over. The planks weren't all nailed down and William removed two of them, tossing them aside as he peered down into the hole.

"William, Mommy said never to go near there," Jonathan said.

"But there's a poor little kitty that's fallen in and needs our help," William said. "Can't you hear it crying?"

"Oh, poor kitty!" Jonathan said.

Harper lunged forward, trying to stop what she knew would happen, but there was nothing she could do. She watched as Jonathan ran to William's side. Just as he came near the edge, William shoved him, sending Jonathan toppling into the well. At the last second, Jonathan grabbed hold of a long pipe that ran across the top of the opening.

"Help, William! Help me!" Jonathan cried. "I'm going to fall!"

"Then fall already!" William shouted. Leaning forward,

he stomped on Jonathan's hand. Jonathan shrieked in agony but didn't let go. Suddenly, the wooden board William was stepping on collapsed, sending him plunging into the well. Their mother came rushing out of the house and covered her mouth with her hands, muffling her screams. She carefully crawled forward on her stomach and dragged Jonathan to safety. Holding on to a hysterical Jonathan, the mother stared down into the well to see William's broken body, his eyes open but unseeing.

"Oh, William," she whispered. Hugging her crying son, she ran to her neighbors, shouting for help.

Harper stood at the edge of the well, staring down at the dead boy. Suddenly, the corpse lunged up at her with a deafening scream. His face was all rage, a contorted mask of hate. His small hands curled into claws that wrapped around Harper's neck, pulling her down into the well. Screaming, falling, never ending.

The sensation of falling was so severe it jolted Harper out of her trancelike state. Her body was covered in sweat.

Harper spent the morning wide awake in her room, shaken by her vision. As soon as she could, she walked to Dayo's house, anxious to see her friend. Her mother had given her a box of chocolates to bring over to the house and a bag of gourmet doggy treats. At first her mother insisted on driving her, but Harper didn't want to wait. She needed to get out of the house. After assuring her mom that she was all right, Harper headed out.

At the door, Mrs. Clayton greeted her with a smile.

"Just in time to be my taste tester for a new cookie recipe," she said.

Harper took a big whiff. "Mmmmmmm, your house always smells so good."

Dayo came down carrying Pumpkin, whose tail wagged as soon as she saw Harper.

"Ooooooh, chocolates!" Dayo said. "Can I have one now?"

"Maybe later," Mrs. Clayton said. "Come taste my molasses-and-ginger marshmallow cookies and tell me what you think."

Dayo pulled a face at Harper. "They're not my favorite," she whispered.

"I heard that," Mrs. Clayton hollered from the kitchen.

Dayo snickered. "So what's up? You okay?" she asked.

Harper sighed. "Dayo, do you really believe in ghosts?"

Her friend nodded vigorously. "Sure do," she said.

"What's not to believe? When people die, not everyone makes it to where they need to be. Some get stuck and some don't want to go. At least, that's what my grandma says." She looked at Harper with widening eyes. "You saw something, didn't you!"

They were at the dining room table where Mrs. Clayton had piled up a plate of cookies and two mugs of hot tea with milk and honey. Dayo put Pumpkin on the floor and sat down, waiting impatiently for her mom to leave the room.

A soft nudge and then a warm wet nose nuzzled against Harper's bare leg. Looking down, she saw Pumpkin sitting at her feet, making puppy eyes at her.

"Pumpkin, I'm so glad to see you feeling better," Harper said, reaching down to pet the little dog.

"She's fine now, she's just been sleeping a lot. But don't let her get any of my cookies! She's been getting way too many treats lately," Mrs. Clayton said. "Between her puppy eyes and her cast, no one can resist her begging."

Harper found herself melting under the cuteness of Pumpkin's pose. "Sorry, Pumpkin, I'm too selfish to share, but you can have one of the special treats I brought later," she said. She took a big bite of her cookie and gave Dayo's mother two enthusiastic thumbs-up.

Before Mrs. Clayton could respond, Dayo made a big irritated noise. "Mom, will you go back into the kitchen? We're trying to talk here."

Mrs. Clayton rolled her eyes and ducked away.

Drumming her fingertips on the tabletop, Dayo glared at Harper. "Well? Tell me what you saw!"

Harper polished off her second cookie with a big swig of her tea before answering.

"Remember when you told me about the families that lived in my house before us? You mentioned that a boy named William had died years ago, right?"

Dayo nodded.

"This is going to sound crazy but I think I've been having visions of him in the house."

"How do you know it's the same William?"

"Because the visions are from a long time ago—I saw how he died."

Dayo gasped as Harper launched into an explanation of what she'd seen. When she was done, Dayo jumped to her feet.

"Wait here," Dayo said. "I'll be right back."

Harper kept eating cookies until Dayo came back with her laptop.

"Let me look at the facts." She searched online for a few minutes before gasping out loud once again. "I don't believe it."

"What is it?" Harper asked.

Dayo turned the laptop screen so Harper could see what it said. Harper read the paragraph Dayo was pointing to and she could barely contain her shock.

> In 1925, the Bellair family moved in and suffered a terrible tragedy when their older son, William, died in an accident. William, 8, and his younger brother, Jonathan, 5, were playing near a boarded-up well when the wooden planks broke. The older Bellair child plunged to his death.

The two girls stared at each other in amazement.

"Harper, if you are seeing visions of the Bellair boys, then that means your house really is haunted."

Both girls shuddered in unison.

Dayo once again jumped to her feet and ran into the kitchen, only to run back with a large empty water bottle.

"We need to get you some more holy water," she said with grim determination.

"Do you really think it will help?" Harper asked.

Her friend nodded. "It will protect you before things can get much worse."

Thinking about Michael, Harper wondered if the worst had already happened.

HARPER'S STUPID DC JOURNAL

Entry #12

Things I hate:

1. *Liars*
2. *That old red fire truck*
3. *Monsters*

The other night I woke up because my room was freezing cold. The first thing I noticed was that my door was open and my bells and little purse from Grandma Lee had fallen off the doorknob. I slammed the door shut when I sensed that I wasn't alone.

In the far corner, I saw a small shape hunched over.

"Michael, is that you?"

There was no answer.

I reached over to turn on my light. The bulb flashed and burned out with a sharp pop. I covered my eyes trying to get rid of the spots that swam before me. Cautiously I stepped forward. A ray of moonlight sent a shadow across the wall, which stopped me in my tracks. The shadow was bizarre and strangely shaped.

"Michael?" I asked again.

I suddenly realized that whoever was in my room wasn't my brother. I started to back away slowly when the figure began to unfold itself, growing long and tall. Its head was still bowed down, but the figure stretched and grew, looming high above my head until I found myself staring at a monster. Its face was that of a corpse, insects twisting in and out of holes in its rotted flesh. It reached out for me with its long clawlike hands.

I screamed and ran for the door, pulling and turning at the knob. But the door wouldn't budge. The creature kept growing until it filled the entire corner of my room, its arms extending slowly toward me even as its head grew larger, dipping lower as it crowded against the ceiling. I turned back to the door and banged on it hard. Over my shoulder I could see razor-sharp claws reaching down, could feel the tips scraping against my back.

"Harper . . ." The monster's voice was raspy and ancient.

My terror was so intense, I wanted to throw up. My heart hammered so hard I thought it would break through my ribs. I tried the door again, but it still wouldn't open. At my feet, I saw the bells and my charms bag. Quickly grabbing the purse, I turned around and flung it right into the monster's face. The monster shrieked so horribly that I fell to the ground, covering my head with my arms.

When I finally lowered my arms, I saw that I was alone in my room. I couldn't tell if it had been real or a dream. But spilled salt, fennel, and pine needles from my charm bag were all over the floor of my bedroom.

THE BASEMENT

Day 8–Monday lunchtime

Harper heard her mom calling everyone to lunch. She was not surprised to come down and see pizza on the table. It was from a chain and tasted more like cardboard with tomato sauce than real New York–style pizza. It didn't even smell good. She thought of how Dayo's house always smelled of the delicious food Mrs. Clayton made, and Harper was filled with envy. Even though her parents didn't cook often, at least in New York there were so many good things to eat.

She looked over to where Michael was eating his pizza. He had his beat-up fire truck on the table. Yuna must have cleaned it up and given it back to him. He sat staring at the truck and eating his pizza like a robot.

A wave of homesickness hit Harper, and with the nightmares, the accidents, and the change in Michael, she had to fight hard to hold back her tears.

"I really hate it here," she whispered.

Kelly, who was looking at her soggy pizza slice with disdain, dropped it on her plate with a disgusted sound.

"We gotta find a decent pizza place here," she said. She looked up to see Harper wiping away the tears from her face. "Hey doughnut cannibal, why don't we try to find a Krispy Kreme later? There's supposed to be one where you can watch the doughnuts move down a conveyor belt and get covered in glaze."

Harper blinked back her tears in surprise. "You'd really take me?"

"Yeah, I need a break, anyway," Kelly said. "We should drive around and explore the neighborhood. There's gotta be better food options around."

"That would be awesome!" Harper was so excited. "And maybe we can find out where Grandma lives and visit her!"

Kelly swiveled her head to see if their mother was around before turning back and pressing her finger to her lips.

"Shush, what's the matter with you? If you get me in trouble, Mom will take away my driving privileges," Kelly said.

Harper deflated.

"Look, I want to see Grandma again, too," Kelly said. "But Mom won't let me drive too far yet since we're in a new city and Grandma is in Maryland."

"I'm sorry," Harper said. She knew her sister was right. "But we can still drive around and look for a Krispy Kreme?"

Harper looked at Michael. Her brother loved doughnuts as much as she did.

"Hey, little buddy, snap out of it! Kelly's gonna take us for doughnuts," she said as she gave him a nudge on his shoulder. All she wanted was to see the old Michael react the way he used to. Instead, he slapped her hand and glared at her.

"I'm not going nowhere with you two boobs," he snarled.

"What did you call me, you little brat?" Kelly snapped at him.

"Buzz off, you fat cow!"

"Why, you nasty little turd! I am so sick of you!"

"I hate you!" he snarled.

Kelly jumped out of her seat and lunged for

Michael, who immediately began screaming, "Mom! Help! She's trying to hurt me!"

Kelly backed off as Yuna came in from her office.

"What's going on here?"

Michael immediately ran to her side and raised his arms to be picked up.

"They're both so mean to me," he whined from the safety of her arms. "They said they wanted to beat me!"

"That's it! Forget about me taking you anywhere," Kelly threw up her hands and stormed out. Harper was disappointed to see Kelly's bad mood return, but she was more disturbed by Michael's behavior.

"Mama, I don't like Kelly," Michael said. "She's a bad girl. Promise me you won't go out with her?"

"I'm not going anywhere today, but I have to do some work," Yuna replied. "Harper, will you take Michael to the library? There's a story-time session this afternoon."

Before Harper could respond, Michael began to scream.

"No, no, no! I won't go! You can't make me!"

"Michael, calm down right now, or you will go straight into a time-out!"

At Yuna's words, Michael started hitting Yuna on

the face and chest. In shock, she put him down. Then he flung himself back and banged his head against the floor.

"Stop it, Michael, don't do that!" Yuna tried to pick him up again, but he kicked at her and continued to bang his head.

"Harper, go get your father! He's in the basement with the contractors."

Harper paused. The basement was the only part of the house she had yet to venture into. If the attic was frightening, the idea of the basement was far worse. If you were locked in the basement, there would be no escape.

"Hurry, Harper!"

With a deep breath, Harper walked to the back of the house where the basement entrance was. The door to the basement was slightly ajar. She peered down at the wooden plank stairs. All she could hear was a loud hammering and drilling sound. Taking a firm grip on the railing, Harper slowly walked down the steps. The basement door swung shut behind her. The farther she went down, the brighter it got. Once in the basement, she saw that the contractors had rigged large work lights in the back room. One of them was hammering some wood beams into place while another was using a drill. Harper spotted her father talking to another man over a pile of large blueprints.

"Dad, Mom needs you right now!" Harper shouted. The noise was too loud; nobody could hear her. Reluctantly, she walked over and tapped her father on the shoulder.

He turned to Harper as the contractor went over to his workers, stopping all the noise. The sudden silence was a relief.

Before Harper could speak, the head contractor interrupted. "Peter, we're going to take a lunch break now and be back in an hour," he said.

"Sure thing. Thanks, guys," her father said before rolling up the blueprints.

"What's up, honey?"

At that moment, the contractors opened the basement door and the noise from Michael's screaming flooded the room.

"Hey, Pete, you might want to come up here," the head contractor shouted. "I think your wife has a situation."

"Be right up," Peter responded, his eyebrows furrowed in concern. "Sorry, honey, can it wait? I need to go upstairs."

"That's what I'm trying to tell you," Harper replied. "Mom needs your help with Michael—now!"

Peter bolted for the stairs. Harper tried to run after him, but when she reached the bottom of the stairs, the basement door slammed shut behind him and suddenly all the lights shut off.

It was pitch-black and unearthly silent. Harper could no longer hear Michael's screams. The only sound she could hear was the rapid-fire beating of her heart and her own belabored breathing. She tried to edge herself up the stairs but she was paralyzed by her own fright. Pressing herself hard against the wall, Harper slid down onto the floor and reached her arms out. Maybe she could crawl up the stairs. But no matter how far she extended her arms, she couldn't feel the bottom step. It made no sense. It should be right there, but it was as if it had disappeared.

The silence was broken by a murmuring sound. Harper sobbed and closed her eyes tight as she felt the chill of the basement deepen. Whispers filled her head and her teeth began to chatter.

Harper opened her eyes and she was no longer in the basement. Moonlight shone through bars of the bird-poop-covered window. She was in the same ugly yellow hospital room from her previous nightmares. Briarly. And then the voices started.

She thinks she's a witch. Dahlia's so weird. She tried to

curse someone. Even her parents don't like her. They sent her away forever. So she killed herself.

Dahlia's Dead. Dead Dahlia. Dead Dahlia.

Dead dead dead dead dead . . .

Harper ran to her door, trying to get out before it was too late. But the door was stuck and wouldn't budge.

A freezing cold filled the room and Harper's breath fanned out in a foggy mist. She stopped screaming immediately. She was no longer alone.

Harper didn't want to look but she couldn't help herself. At the foot of the bed stood a figure. Her long dark-brown hair hung like a dirty cloud around her neck and she wore the faded blue uniform of every Briarly patient. Except hers was covered with dark stains that could only be blood.

But the worst part was that her neck was broken, leaving her head hanging at a right angle from her body. Dahlia stood staring at Harper out of her sideways face, her mouth gaping and eyes burning a feverish yellow.

Nobody loves you. Nobody cares about you. Your own mother hates you.

Harper squeezed her eyes shut, but she couldn't block out the voice.

Your mother thinks you're crazy. Your mother doesn't

want you anymore. She wants you to stay here. You can never go home.

The voice morphed into an image of Harper's mother looking angry and bitter. The words were now coming out of Yuna's mouth.

I wish you were never born. Our family would be perfect if it weren't for you.

Harper choked on helpless tears.

"No, Mom, don't say that," Harper begged.

You've been such a disappointment to me.

"No, you're not real," she said. "I don't believe you." Harper shook her head hard.

The vision of her mom continued to speak those horrible words. *I've never loved you.*

Her mom would never say that, would she?

Nobody loves you. Nobody cares about you.

"My dad loves me," Harper whispered.

The voice seemed to pause and then continued.

Your dad left you. He doesn't care about you. He doesn't want to see you anymore. He ran away. He ran away from us. He left us because of you.

Harper opened her eyes and glared at Dahlia.

"No, he didn't! And you're not my mom!" she yelled. "This is about you, Dahlia, not me. Your mother left you here. Your dad left you, not mine.

Maybe nobody loved you, Dahlia, but my parents love me!"

The whispering stopped. But then Dahlia reappeared, screaming, her sideways face a distortion of humanity. In a rage, Dahlia attacked and flung Harper's body across the room like a rag doll. As she lay dazed on the floor, she watched as Dahlia climbed spider-like up the wall and onto the ceiling right above her. She came charging down at full speed. Harper felt a vise grip on the back of her neck that whipped her straight up into the air and slammed her into the high ceiling. It held her there for a long painful moment and then released her suddenly.

Harper crashed down, her arms taking the brunt of the fall as they snapped back in excruciating pain. The side of her face bounced hard against the carpeted floor.

She could hear herself screaming, but as if it was from far away. Her father was there hugging her tight, apologizing for leaving her behind. At first she thought he was talking about Briarly. But then she realized where she was. She was in the basement. She was safe—she was going to be okay. And now she finally knew what had happened to her in Briarly.

HARPER'S STUPID DC JOURNAL

Entry #13

Things I hate:

1. *The basement*

MEMORIES

Day 8–Monday night

Harper was sitting on the bench in the foyer again, staring at the mirror. Her room hadn't felt safe since the terrifying monster vision and she might never step foot into the basement ever again. This was the only part of the house that felt safe to her these days.

After he came back to the basement, her father had carried Harper upstairs while she was still in hysterics. Her mother had blamed him for leaving her in the dark. They had no idea that it was more than that. Harper didn't want to tell them. What was she supposed to say? That she remembered what had happened at Briarly? That ghosts were real and one tried to kill her? If she were to tell her parents that, especially her mother, they might send her right back to the hospital.

Her chest felt like it was on fire and she was hyperventilating. She wrapped her shaking arms around herself and tried to calm down. Her head began to throb. There were voices whispering all around her. She squeezed her eyes tight and covered her ears, but the voices were inside of her head.

Come play with me, we're gonna be best friends!

We'll be friends forever.

So many different voices. She couldn't tell them apart.

I've been so lonely.

Stay with me!

Don't listen to them. You're meant to be with me.

The moonlight was streaming in through the narrow windows on both sides of the front door. The reflections of light danced across the mirror, catching her attention. Harper was mesmerized by the little sparks of brilliant color that whirled in front of her. They were soothing; they caused most of the voices to fade away, except for one.

Harper! I'm here.

She knew that voice. It was so familiar. It was

warm. It was a voice she had once loved. Memories floated around the edges of her thoughts.

Harper, I'm here! Open your eyes and see with your heart.

She could feel the breath of someone talking right into her ear. She jumped in shock and pressed herself against the wall. There was no one around and yet the voice had been right next to her.

Open your eyes!

The voice grew to a shout that echoed in Harper's ears, making them ring so hard she shivered involuntarily. She clapped her hands over her ears as they began to throb in pain. Just when she thought she could no longer stand the pain, there was a bright flash of light that blinded her. All she could see was blank whiteness.

And then a rush of images surged through Harper's brain, so fast and overwhelming, she couldn't make any sense of them.

It was all coming back to her. The memories sent her into the past to relive it all in horrifying detail. Scenes flew by in reverse until that moment in the foyer when she was four. The moment she met Rose.

Harper opened her eyes and stood straight. She walked up close to the foyer mirror and stared into the darkness at her reflection. Now everything was so clear. She finally had found the missing jigsaw piece of her memories.

"Rose," she whispered. "I remember you. I remember everything."

Just then, like the first time, the girl in the mirror appeared.

HARPER'S STUPID DC JOURNAL

Entry #14

Things I hate:

1. *All the time I've lost with Rose*
2. *Now that I'm beginning to remember things again, there are some memories that are coming in so clear. Like the day Grandma Lee bought the mirror for us when I was four years old.*

"It's for Harper," she said.

I was so excited to hang it in my room, but my parents explained that it was too big and had to stay in the foyer.

And of course once I met Rose, the mirror became my most favorite thing in the whole world. I remember watching Snow White and the Seven Dwarves *and thinking that the queen had a bad mirror. Mine was clearly so much better. And more fun, too.*

Playing hide-and-seek with Rose was my most favorite thing in the world, even though it should've been unfair. I mean, who hides better than a ghost? But Rose would always leave me hints. Like if she hid behind the curtains, she'd shimmer so I could see the sparkles around the window. Or if she was in the closet, little dots of light would dance in the air in front of the door. At night, we'd huddle in bed together and read books under the covers with a flashlight. She was the best friend I could ever have. The only thing she couldn't do was leave the house. She could only move about within the building where her mirror was located.

I once asked Rose how she came to be in our mirror, and she told me about how she'd died and became trapped there. The story made me cry.

When Rose was fifteen, she was diagnosed with tuberculosis. In those days, it was called consumption because the disease, which was almost always fatal, seemed to consume its victims, wasting them away to nothing until they died. Because the sun hurt Rose's eyes, her mother installed heavy drapes in her room, blocking all light out. The room was a tomb except for the flickering of the candlelight reflected in her bedroom mirror, the same mirror that now hung in our foyer. When Rose had a good day, her mother would sit her in front of that mirror, brushing her hair, telling her how beautiful she was, how she couldn't live without her.

The day Rose died, her spirit became stuck in that heavy grief-stricken room. Her mother was inconsolable and kept the curtains drawn. There was no light for Rose's spirit to follow. So she found herself floating into the mirror, where the flickering lights of the candles shone the brightest. Once inside the mirror, she became bonded to it, unable to stray far from it for very long, always subject to go where it went. Sadly, her mother never looked at the mirror ever again, but even if she had, Rose wasn't sure she would have noticed her there.

I promised Rose that I would always look in the mirror for her. Even when my memory was gone, my attachment to the mirror had remained strong. That's how much she has always meant to me. I missed her even when I couldn't remember her.

HARPER'S AURA

Day 8—Monday night, continued

"Harper, I've been so worried about you!" Rose rushed out of the mirror and grabbed Harper in a ghostly embrace that felt like being squished between soft clouds. "I thought you would never remember me again!"

The rush of love and affection that filled Harper caused her to laugh with joy. "Rose, I've missed you so much and I didn't even know it!"

"And how do you think I felt? I could see you every day but never talk to you," Rose said. "It was like going back to the dark days."

Harper nodded solemnly. She remembered that the dark days were what they called the time before they became friends. For Rose had never left the mirror until the day she'd saved Harper.

"I've felt helpless," Rose said with a soft sob. "This house is so evil. I've been investigating and finding out so many things. I tried to share them with you."

Harper's mouth dropped open. "The visions about William and the house I've been having! That was you?"

Rose nodded. "They're old memories from this house. When you were sleeping or just daydreaming, I could see your aura a little more clearly. And so I could share the visions because they are powerfully rooted to this house."

"What's an aura?" Harper asked.

"It's the energy field that surrounds every living creature," Rose said. "It is like a magnetic call to any spiritual being in your immediate area. Yours was an intensely bright and brilliant silvery-white. But ever since your accident, it's been completely muted and dulled to a faint light blue."

"My aura," Harper breathed. "That's why I can see ghosts?"

"No, your aura is why they are attracted to you," Rose said, "like moths to a flame. Your aura is so strong that being near you feels almost like being alive again. Your ability to see and talk to ghosts is something different."

"How is that?"

Rose shrugged. "I don't know but it's a very rare gift."

"What do they want with my light?" Harper thought about Dahlia and shuddered. "Why do they want to hurt me?"

"Some spirits are gentle and would never harm anyone. But there are also unhappy spirits and those that are just evil. They will hurt you or, worse, want to take over your body so they can live again. It's because you have such a strong aura. That's why you can't let them into your mind. It's too dangerous."

Rose's words triggered another memory of the blond, gray-eyed little girl whose hair glowed white with electricity.

"The fire at the school," Harper blurted out in shock. "My mom was right. It really was my fault! I let her in."

"No, don't blame yourself. It was the ghost girl Maddie's fault," Rose said. "You didn't want to let her in. She took over your body and started the fire. That was the last thing you told me before they sent you to Briarly. And when you came back, you'd forgotten me."

Harper knew why she'd set the fire now. She'd been left in the art room alone while the teacher went to check on a disturbance in the hallway. In those few minutes, she'd been terrorized by Maddie until finally Maddie had taken control of her body and set the room on fire. But when Harper was rescued from the burning room, nobody else was there.

Rose nodded. "You can't blame them, really. Very few people can actually see ghosts, and even fewer of them can communicate with us."

"Lucky me," Harper grouched.

Rose looked hurt.

"Oh no, Rose, I didn't mean you!" Harper rushed to apologize. "I just meant the ones that try to hurt me, like the ghost at Briarly."

"What happened there? Will you tell me?"

"The ghost of a girl named Dahlia haunted my room," Harper said. "She was so angry and full of hate. But the worst part of all was how strong she was."

"Angry ghosts feed on fear," Rose said. "The more frightened you were, the stronger she would grow."

Harper shuddered. "She almost killed me."

Rose's form shimmered in distress. "Harper, you're not safe here, either. I've been so worried for you."

Harper remembered how, after being shoved down the stairs, she felt something stop her descent. "It was you that saved me from falling all the way down the stairs!"

Rose nodded. "I wanted to do more, but I was afraid."

"Of the ghosts?"

Rose shook her head. "No, of the house. There's something really wrong with this place."

"What is it?"

"I don't know. But it's old. Older than the ghost boy."

The ghost boy. William. Billy.

She turned to Rose with a terrible fear growing in the pit of her stomach. Her visions of the evil William leaped into her mind.

"Rose, I'm afraid for my brother," she started. "All this time Michael has been talking about an imaginary friend, Billy. But he isn't imaginary, is he? Billy is actually the ghost of William."

Rose nodded again. "Your brother is in serious danger."

HARPER'S STUPID DC JOURNAL

Entry #15

Things I hate:

1. Being possessed by an evil spirit

I know how terrible it is to feel trapped in your own body. It's what happened to me before the fire was started.

I remember it all now. How my art teacher, Mr. Manning, always thought I was a troublemaker in class. How the other kids all thought I was weird and would stare at me.

"Harper's talking to herself again," they'd whisper loudly, giggling. Even Mr. Manning would stop what he was doing and glare at me.

I would put my head down, not only to avoid their stares, but to ignore the girl that nobody else could see. I would beg her to leave me alone, but she wouldn't listen. She would vanish and reappear, startling me all the time. She'd shove my pencils off the desk, send my papers flying, and spill paint all over my hands. She would not stop bothering me.

Play with me.

Play with me now!

It was the beginning of sixth grade and I'd only been in art class for a few days when I first met Maddie. She was the ghost of a young girl who'd died fifty years earlier in a fire at the school. I found this out when I overheard the administrators in the front office talking in hushed voices about the old fire and the poor girl who had been killed. That was Maddie.

She'd been friendly at first, painfully happy to have someone to talk to. It was the first time since she'd died that she'd had a conversation with anyone. And she seemed so desperate to have a friend.

But then, after a few weeks, she became more and more aggressive. She would try to take over my body. I would feel a sudden hard pressure at the back of my head and it would hurt so much. Rose told me never to let the ghost girl gain control of me but it was getting harder and harder to fight her. Rose said it was because the ghost was jealous that I was alive. Maddie wanted to live again, too, or take me down with her.

On the day of the fire, she was hostile.

Come on, Harper, I just want to paint something!

"Leave me alone, Maddie," I whispered.

In retaliation, she sent my pencil case flying across the room.

"That's it, Harper—you get detention," Mr. Manning said. "Stay after class."

I could feel my face burning red with embarrassment as everyone smirked and laughed at me, even Maddie. I didn't know what to do, except to try to ignore her, even though that never worked.

Harper, why won't you play with me? *Maddie kept whining. I felt her yank my hair hard. I tried not to cry as she started to pull, poke, and pinch me all over my body, but it was hard. I was afraid of what she would do to me. I couldn't understand how someone with no physical body could cause so much pain. Then a sudden poke into my brain gave me such a blinding headache that I felt like vomiting. I dropped my head onto my desk and closed my eyes until the bell rang.*

I listened to the scraping of chairs, the shuffling feet, and lively chatter as the other students left class. When the room was quiet, I heard the heavy footsteps of the teacher approach my desk and I sat up.

"Harper," Mr. Manning said. "You and I are going down to the principal's office in a few minutes to have a chat about your disruptive behavior. This time we are going to have to call your parents in. Understood?"

"Yes sir," I muttered. I was relieved to be leaving the art class. Maybe I could ask my parents to switch me to another room.

Just then, there was a loud disturbance from the hallway. We could hear screaming and banging.

"Stay in your seat and don't move," Mr. Manning said as he walked out of the room.

I wanted to shout at him not to leave me alone with her, but as soon as Mr. Manning left, Maddie appeared, sitting on my desk. Let's play now!

I leaped to my feet and backed away. There was an intensity to Maddie that was almost electric. Dangerous.

"Maddie, you have to leave me alone," I said. "You're always getting me in trouble."

Sparks seemed to leap out of her ghostly body. Maddie's blond hair had turned white, while her gray eyes gleamed with a silverish cast.

Harper, you're my only friend. I just want to play with you. *Maddie's body began to drift higher, her form seemed made of pure electricity.*

Fright sent me running for the door. I knew I was in a lot of trouble. Papers flew up in the air and whirled around like a mini tornado, while pencils and crayons pelted me from all directions. Before I could reach the door, Maddie grabbed me by the hair and dragged me back into the middle of the room.

I started screaming, hoping a teacher would come in, but midshout I suddenly remembered Rose's words and realized my mistake. Rose said that terror fueled spirits, making them more powerful. But it was too late: Maddie's electrified form dove straight into my mouth. It felt as if I was being electrocuted. I wanted to fight for control over my body, but I didn't know what to do. I was paralyzed both inside and out. And then Maddie took over. She made me rise to my feet. I was trapped. All I could hear were Maddie's thoughts in my head. Nothing I was doing anymore was me. I was a puppet.

Fire fire fire . . .

Maddie was heading straight for the supply closet where Mr. Manning kept the butane torches. It was locked but

Maddie forced me to slam my body into the door several times. Harder and harder, until the door was forced open, the wood around the doorknob splintering. It was as if Maddie had given my body superhuman strength.

Maddie, stop! *I pleaded, but she ignored me. She just kept chanting* fire fire fire *over and over in a singsong way. Now that she was in my head, I could see into her mind, into her past. She was a firebug. A pyromaniac. The fire she died in? She started it herself. I was in so much trouble.*

I tried to resist, but she made my body reach for the butane torch and forced me to head straight for the windows where the papier-mâché projects had been set out to dry. Some were painted, some were still half constructed, but they were all made from newspaper strips and glue. The most flammable stuff in the world.

Maddie pushed the button that ignited the torch and then turned the knob to create a huge flame. She held the flame to the closest project, cackling with glee when it erupted into flames. I could only watch in horror as my own hand set it on fire.

Inside my mind, I was caught in a battle for control. I was screaming internally, over and over again. All my energy was now focused on keeping my arm in place, and moving my thumb off the button that controlled the flame.

Get out! *My scream echoed in my head and I could feel Maddie's power over me weaken. My brain felt like it was going to explode. With one last huge burst of energy, I took control of my arm and threw the torch across the room. The fire was spreading so quickly that all the projects in the windows were ablaze and fire alarms had begun to ring.*

"Get out now!" I shouted out loud this time. I pushed all my thoughts against Maddie's presence. I was so angry, I let my rage fight against her willpower and finally forced Maddie out of my body. The relief was instantaneous. The pressure inside my head was gone. The rage left me and I was overwhelmed by exhaustion. The last thing I remember was falling to the ground, watching the billowing smoke fill the room.

A RAT IN THE HOUSE

Day 9—Early Tuesday morning

Rose and Harper had spent most of the night in the foyer, whispering to each other so no one else could hear them. Harper was both too excited and too anxious to sleep and there was so much to talk about. They were both startled when they heard piercing screams coming from upstairs. Harper ran up as her parents reached Kelly's room. Harper followed them in and found her sister in hysterics. There was a dead mouse lying on the pillow in her bed.

"I felt something on my hair and I woke up and I found that thing *in my face*!"

Harper couldn't even look at it. She was horribly afraid of all rodents.

"Does that mean there are probably more mice in our house, Dad?" Harper asked. It was her worst nightmare. She shivered at the thought and wanted to get off the floor; she could almost feel them running over her feet.

"Did it crawl up and die in her bed?" Yuna asked, her face distorted in disgust.

Peter turned away from Kelly so she couldn't see his troubled face. He was holding the dead mouse wrapped in toilet paper. "I don't think so," he said in a low voice.

"Oh gross," Yuna said. "There's blood on its head. How in the world could it have gotten up into Kelly's bed?"

"Blood?" Kelly sputtered. "You mean someone killed it and put it on my bed?"

Kelly turned to Harper with a horrified expression. "Did you do this to me? Was it because I wouldn't drive you to Krispy Kreme?"

Harper's mouth gaped open at Kelly's accusation. She couldn't believe what she was hearing.

"There's no way Harper could do that," Peter responded sharply. "She could never hurt anything.

Not to mention the fact that she has a serious mouse phobia."

"Then who? Who would do this to me?"

Harper could feel her anger rising at the accusation. "Maybe you did this to yourself for attention!"

"Get out of my room!" Kelly shouted.

Harper fled to her own bedroom and slammed the door. The idea of killing a living creature would be horrifying, even if she wasn't deathly afraid of rodents. Just the thought of being anywhere near a mouse made Harper sick to her stomach. This was an all-time low, even for Kelly.

There was a time when Harper and Kelly had been close. She wasn't sure what had happened. She kept blaming high school, but this rift started before then. When they were young, Kelly would always accuse Harper of lying and making things up. The older they got, the more it felt like they were drifting too far apart. Was it a bad thing if sisters weren't friends? At least she had Michael, who, she realized, hadn't come out of his room at all after Kelly's screams.

Harper silently opened her door and stuck her head out into the hallway. From her viewpoint, she could see Michael's door was ajar and he was staring at Kelly's room with a dead expression on his face. He turned his head and caught Harper's eye.

His gaze held hers for such a long time, Harper became afraid of him.

And then without a word, he closed his door.

Day 9—Later Tuesday morning

Tired from a long sleepless night, Harper napped until late morning. When she woke up, Rose was floating at the foot of her bed.

"You're still here!" Harper said in relief. "I was worried that it was all a dream."

Rose smiled. "Of course I'm still here. But you have to replace your salt talisman." She pointed at the empty pouch on the floor near the door.

"My charms bag from my grandma? Why?" Harper asked.

"Your grandmother made it specifically to keep evil spirits away. I remember her saying that as she put them all over your old home. When combined with the bells, they make a very powerful talisman that will protect you. Now that your aura is so bright again, you're more of a target than before."

"Grandma Lee? How did she know to do that?"

Rose shrugged. "I remember thinking this lady knows what she's doing. But here in this house, you're the only one who remembered to use it."

"But the charm bag and bells don't bother you?" Harper asked.

Rose shook her head. "I don't really like them, but they don't keep me out."

Harper scratched her head. "Is that because you're a good ghost?"

"I don't know, but I would never hurt you."

Harper started changing out of her pajamas when she had another thought.

"Rose, if Michael was talking to William this whole time, then that means he is like me," she said. "Has Michael seen you? Have you talked to him?"

"No. His ability didn't manifest until you moved into this house. By the time I realized, he was already too close with William for me to show myself. So I've been hiding deep in my mirror, hoping you would remember."

"Has William possessed Michael completely now?" Harper asked in distress.

Rose nodded urgently. "You have to help him. Before it's too late."

"But I've never been able to stop a ghost before,"

Harper said. The memories of Dahlia and Maddie made her shudder. "They're too strong for me."

"You're so powerful, Harper," Rose replied. "Maddie tried to possess you and you were able to fight her off. You broke her control. Now you have to do it for your brother."

For a moment, Harper panicked. The idea of fighting ghosts made her want to run screaming out of the house. But the thought of her baby brother kept her focused. She knew how scary it was to be possessed. She had to help him.

"What do I do?"

"I'm not sure. William is evil—that I know. I've been snooping around the house catching glimpses of past memories. And what I've seen has worried me," Rose said.

"Glimpses?"

"Like this," Rose said as she beckoned Harper. She drifted down the stairs and into the kitchen. Harper followed her glowing form and bright-red hair. Once in the kitchen, Rose touched Harper's face with one hand and the wall with the other.

Immediately Harper was in another time and place. It was daytime and she was no longer in the present. Their new modern kitchen was gone and instead they stood in a room out of an old black-and-white television show. The wallpaper was white and covered in big red roses and the appliances were shiny white new versions of antiques.

This transformation took place in the space of a heartbeat, as Harper immediately spotted William and his brother sitting at the kitchen table, drawing on scraps of paper while their mother was busy cooking. She pulled a large roast from the oven and left it on the countertop just as the doorbell rang.

"Let me answer that. You boys stay away from the oven," she said, wiping her hands on her apron before taking it off. "It's very hot."

As soon as she left, William walked over to the oven.

"Hey!" William said. "She left the cookies out!"

Jonathan smiled in glee. "I want one!"

He ran toward William, but right as he came upon the oven, William swung the door open, causing him to trip and fall onto the inside of the hot metal door.

Jonathan shrieked in pain as his small hands began to blister. William smiled.

The screams faded along with the memory as Rose let go of the wall.

"He's a monster," Harper whispered.

Rose pressed a finger to her lips and gestured

Harper to the back of the house where her parents had set up their home office. Harper went into the room, turned on the light, and closed the door.

"He usually stays upstairs but I don't want to risk William overhearing us," Rose said.

"We're safe here?"

Rose nodded. "He never comes in here. He avoids this room like the plague."

"I wonder what this room was before," Harper said.

Rose placed her hand on the wall and touched Harper again. The past version of the room appeared. Right away, Harper noticed a large crucifix hanging on the wall with a family shrine on the table beneath it. The shrine had a small statue of the Virgin Mary, numerous candles of various sizes, several rosaries, a leather-bound Bible, and a few flasks containing clear liquid. Holy water, Harper thought. The rest of the room was simple and cozy with two armchairs, a small wooden coffee table, and a basket filled with what looked like knitting supplies. Once Rose let go, they were back in her parents' modern office.

"It was their prayer room," Harper said.

"Holy water," Rose said. "We could use that on William."

"I have a bottle in my room," Harper said. "Dayo gave it to me."

"Okay, then. You say a prayer of exorcism and pour the water over him," Rose said. "But I remember hearing that only a priest experienced with exorcisms can do that."

"Well, that's no good," Harper said. "What if I mess up? I might make it worse."

Rose made a helpless gesture with her hands.

"Then what do I do with the holy water?" Harper asked.

"We should sprinkle some in all the rooms," Rose said.

Harper sighed. Dayo had said the same thing. "Okay, but I'm gonna start in Michael's room and see what happens."

Rose looked worried.

"Bad idea?" Harper asked.

"That ghost really scares me," Rose said. "Be careful, Harper."

"I will, don't worry."

Harper went back to her room, finished getting ready, brushed her teeth, washed her face, and then grabbed the holy water. She knocked on Michael's door and entered without waiting for a response.

Michael sat in the middle of the room, staring into nothingness. She immediately began to sprinkle holy water in the four corners of the room, walking around Michael. The temperature in the room began to cool rapidly and the air felt heavy and oppressive, as if something big and scary was breathing down her neck.

"Harper, what are you doing?" Michael said, his voice monotone. His deadened gaze followed Harper as she circled the room.

Harper forced herself to ignore the change in the room and knelt in front of him, showing him the bottle. "I'm blessing the house with this holy water Dayo gave me," she said.

With a quick movement, she shook some holy water in Michael's direction.

He recoiled with a curled lip and hissed at her. Harper fell back, frightened by his expression. His face had changed into something distorted and not human. It wasn't William's face, but it wasn't Michael's, either.

"Don't do that," he said, his voice monotonous again. "I don't like it."

Harper tried for a lighthearted expression. "Like what? This?" She sprinkled some more holy water at Michael, this time hitting the side of his face.

At that moment, his expression changed again, to one she knew and loved. "Harper, don't do that! He doesn't like it," Michael said. His eyes were wide and filled with light.

"Who doesn't like it?" Harper asked as Michael's eyes went dark again.

He leaped to his feet and punched Harper hard on the chest, knocking her flat on her back. The small bottle spilled onto the area rug, making a dark stain. Michael jumped onto her stomach and began hitting her as hard as he could. Harper let out a shout of alarm, trying to hold him back but finding him much stronger than a four-year-old should be. Even with the pain of the beating, Harper was more sensitive to the feeling of the house itself. The house was angry, and it was bearing down on her.

Suddenly their mother appeared, pulling Michael off her.

"Michael, stop it!"

In Yuna's arms, he went limp and began to cry. "She hit me first," he said.

"No I didn't," Harper said. "He attacked me!"

"Baloney! You ugly hag!"

"Michael, you do not hit your sister and you do not talk like that in this house," Yuna said sharply. "Apologize at once."

"I didn't do nothing!"

"Michael . . ."

The boy who was not Michael crossed his arms and shook his head furiously.

Yuna sighed and put him down. "All right, come with me. I'm making lunch."

"Oh swell, I want a hot dog."

"We're having pasta," Yuna responded as she tried to move him toward the stairs.

The boy stopped dead in his tracks and glared at Yuna. "I said I wanna hot dog!"

"We don't have any hot dogs."

Harper could see her mother was angry and perplexed.

"You get me a hot dog or I'm gonna throw a fit!"

"Then you're going to have a time-out until you learn how to speak in a respectful manner," Yuna responded.

With a loud, outraged shriek, Michael threw himself on the ground and began to have a temper tantrum.

Harper scrambled to her feet, desperate to get away from the shrieking boy.

She sped down the stairs and to the mirror. The house felt like it wanted to swallow her whole. Like it wanted to crush her and make her disappear. Harper stood in front of the mirror and called to Rose, but her friend didn't appear. Instead Rose's voice whispered in her mind.

Harper, something is wrong. It's not safe for you in the house right now. You need to get out!

At that moment, her father came in and heard the screaming from upstairs.

"Michael again?" he asked with a frown.

Harper nodded, putting on her shoes. "I'm going over to Dayo's. I can't take this right now."

Peter sighed, his eyes filled with worry. "I don't blame you, honey."

And before he could change his mind, Harper ran out the door.

HARPER'S STUPID DC JOURNAL

Entry #16

Things I hate:

1. *Billy, aka William Bellair, aka evil ghost boy*

I hate fighting, but I'm gonna have to do some serious ghost-butt kicking to save my brother. I can't let that ghost take control of Michael. Fact—The ghost of William Bellair is a no-good, rotten jerk. He was a bad kid when he was alive, but he is really evil now that he's a ghost. Poor Michael. He must be so scared. This is my fault. If I hadn't forgotten Rose and Briarly, I could have seen William that first night and stopped him somehow.

Now I have to help Michael no matter what. I'll do whatever it takes to save my brother. Even if it's the last thing I do.

SEEKING A SPIRITUAL ADVISER

Day 9–Tuesday afternoon

The sensation of danger stayed with Harper all the way to Dayo's house. It was as if Dayo could sense her presence, for the minute Harper arrived, the front door opened and Dayo came out with Pumpkin on her leash.

Pumpkin barked happily and limped over to Harper on her cast.

"Hey! I was just thinking about you," Dayo said with a big smile. "What's happening in the house?"

Something about seeing Dayo's smiling face made Harper feel calmer, less scared. It was such a relief to be around her and feel normal. She could breathe again without feeling her chest constrict with fear.

Harper wanted to tell Dayo everything, but she was afraid of what her friend might think. Believing in ghosts was one thing, but saying she had a long-lost best friend who was a ghost? That her little brother was being possessed by the ghost of an evil boy? Even she found it kind of hard to believe.

"I had another vision of that boy who died in the house," Harper confided.

Dayo's eyes widened. "Tell me everything!"

They sat on the front stoop as Harper filled Dayo in on what she had seen. As she talked, Harper could feel her anxiety and fear rising once again.

"I don't know what to do," Harper said.

"This is bad," Dayo said. "Maybe we can ask Father Hurley to come and perform an exorcism."

Harper immediately shook her head. "I don't think that's going to happen. My parents don't believe in ghosts at all, especially my mom."

"But we have to do something!" Dayo looked worried.

Harper was startled to hear her use *we*. It made her almost teary to have a friend like Dayo that she could rely on.

"Thank you for believing me," she said. "You're the first real, alive friend I've ever had."

Dayo gave Harper a hug. "I don't know what other friend you can have but an alive one, but I'm going to help you. Don't worry. We'll figure something out. And if the ghost gets too scary, you can always come stay with me."

Harper glanced wistfully at Dayo's house. "I would love to."

"Anytime!" Dayo exclaimed. "Now let's get to work," she said. She stood up and ushered both Harper and Pumpkin into the house. "We've got research to do!"

"Research?" Harper asked.

"Yeah, maybe we can figure out what William really wants, so that we can send him away."

Half an hour later, the girls were in Dayo's room, comparing their notes.

"Look at this, Harper," said Dayo. "Every time something bad happened in your house, there was a little boy living there."

She circled several names on the papers. "The Bellairs, the Jacobs, and the McCarthys all had a young son that died, almost died, or got sick."

"Well, that makes sense," Harper said. "I think William wants a playmate—someone to take his little brother's place. Although . . ."

Harper was thinking about what Rose had said.

That there was something wrong in the house. Something that was older than the ghost boy. She would have to ask Rose what she meant by that.

"What?" Dayo asked, looking at her expectantly.

"William was the first boy who died in the house after Grady vanished, right?"

Dayo nodded. "The house was empty for a while and then the Bellairs bought it in 1925."

"What if William isn't the only ghost in the house?"

Dayo looked surprised. "Who do you think? Old man Grady? But that doesn't make any sense. Why would he only attack little boys? I would think he'd go after the adults in the house."

Relieved, Harper sat back. "Yeah, you're right. It has to be just William. So about his little brother . . ."

"Hmmmm, but didn't he bully him?" Dayo asked. "In fact, you said he tried to kill him. So that can't be the reason."

"What, then?" Harper asked.

Dayo shook her head. "Let's keep looking. There's a forty-year period where nothing is reported at all while the Richmonds were there. It says their only daughter sold the house in 1965."

"Great!" Harper snorted. "A sexist ghost who hates girls."

But then she thought back to how he acted around her mother. How clingy and adoring he was. "Or wait. William didn't bother the Richmond's daughter because she was a girl."

Harper grabbed Dayo's notes, looking for something she remembered Dayo reading. "Here it is! Mrs. McCarthy pled not guilty by reason of insanity because she claimed that her son had been possessed by an evil spirit and she was only trying to save him."

Dayo gasped. "William wants to live again by taking over your brother's body." Dayo shuddered at her words. "Then he's really in danger!"

Harper didn't tell Dayo that she thought William was already trying to possess Michael.

Harper, don't do that! He doesn't like it.

She knew that it was the real Michael who'd said that. He was still in there. She had to save him. But how? Harper felt so helpless.

Mrs. Clayton called the girls down to lunch.

"It's jerk chicken with rice and callaloo, which are delicious Jamaican stewed greens," Dayo said. "You should stay."

"I have to get home," Harper said.

Dayo patted her on the shoulder. "You gotta eat if you're gonna be fighting evil spirits."

Harper was surprised into a laugh. "Yeah, okay. Besides, it sure smells good."

After a delicious meal, Harper went back home to find Rose in her mirror.

"So, you have to tell me what happened before," she said. "Why did you want me to leave?"

Rose was positioned deeper in the mirror. "I'll meet you in your room."

Up in her room, Rose was already waiting for her. Harper closed the door.

"When you spilled the holy water, I felt the whole house shift—it was shaking with rage."

"William can do that?"

"I don't know," Rose said. "That's what troubles me."

"Earlier you said there was something wrong with the house. What did you mean by that?"

The ghost girl fluttered about the room in distress. "At first I thought it was just William. But ever since William has possessed Michael . . ."

"Don't say that!" Harper interrupted.

"Sorry, but ever since then, I just felt something different in the house," Rose said. "Like the house is waiting for something."

"Waiting for what?"

"For William to possess Michael completely."

Harper was stunned. "No, that can't happen. He can't do that."

"There's nothing we can do," Rose said. "We need professional help."

"Oh great, let me call the Ghostbusters, I'm sure they make house calls." Harper collapsed onto her bed and covered her face with her pillow, trying not to scream.

"No, I'm serious. We need a spiritual adviser," Rose said.

Harper sat up. "What's that?"

"I remember my mom talking to her friends about spiritual advisers who could commune with the dead—they would force them to leave the living alone," Rose said. "The problem was finding a real spiritual adviser and not a fake one."

"Well, how'm I supposed to do that?"

"Harper, you can speak to ghosts. I think that's where you start. Go to a cemetery, ask them for help."

Harper shuddered. "But what if I find a bad ghost like Maddie or Dahlia?"

"If you want to save your brother, what choice do you have? Besides, you should be fine at the cemetery," she said. "The ghosts that linger there are only attached to the memories of their loved ones. They aren't the dangerous ones . . . usually."

"I wish you could come with me," Harper said.

The ghost girl frowned unhappily. "Me too," she sighed. "Stupid mirror."

No matter how hard she tried, Rose couldn't stray far from her mirror. It was her own personal prison.

Harper sighed. "So when should I go?"

HARPER'S STUPID DC JOURNAL

Entry #17

Things I hate:

1. *Cemeteries at nighttime*

I have this vivid memory of being five years old and playing in a cemetery. It was an old church with a graveyard somewhere in New Jersey. My parents had stopped by because there was some farmers' market next door. I was bored with the market so I had wandered over to the cemetery to chase butterflies. I remember playing tag with some kids, weaving in and out of the tombstones. When my parents found me, I was laughing and running around, having a grand old time. As we left, I waved good-bye to my friends. My parents thought I was waving to the stray cats. They never saw the ghosts of the dead kids that were my friends for that day.

THE CEMETERY

Day 9–Tuesday night

Dusk wasn't until nearly nine p.m. The only way Harper would be able to leave was if she sneaked out without anyone seeing her. She'd left her bike hidden by the side of the house. Her dad wasn't home from work yet, and her mom always disappeared into her office at nine p.m.

Harper would have to wait until then to leave and ride down to Our Lady of Mercy in the dark. Would she even be able to find it? Shaking her mind free of any negative thoughts, Harper plotted out her moves and waited.

Sneaking out was far easier than Harper thought it would be. Now she just had to hope that she wouldn't get caught sneaking back in.

The cemetery was the last place most people would want to be after dark, Harper included, but tonight she wove her way through the headstones, seeking out the dead.

Our Lady of Mercy was a picturesque church with a very nice graveyard, beautifully tended and kept in pristine condition. But it was amazing how different it was at nighttime. The darkness caused the delicate dogwood and magnificent maple trees to take on a sinister cast, while the statues of weeping angels became shadowy omens of danger. The large willow tree with its flowing branches was no longer a safe haven, but a menacing presence alive with evil power.

A sudden rustling in the nearby bushes made Harper jump, and her heart thumped painfully as a small brown bunny scurried past her. She wanted to go home. Thoughts of Dahlia and Maddie and even William threatened to overwhelm her, but the fear of losing her brother strengthened her resolve. She loved her brother. She had to save him before William took him over completely.

Stopping in front of a tombstone, Harper took a deep breath and sat on the grass. Rose had told her to try to open all of her senses so that she could access the spirit realm. But how? Maybe through meditation or yoga? She'd once seen Grandma Lee meditate. At first Harper had thought she was sleeping, but her grandmother's lips had been moving for the entire half hour.

Harper decided to try it. She remembered a scene from one of her favorite movies, *Kung Fu Panda*, where Shifu, the red panda kung fu master, had been meditating and chanting "inner peace." Her sister mocked the film all the time. After all *shifu* meant "master," so calling him "Master Shifu" was the equivalent of calling him "master master." Like when Starbucks sells "Chai tea" even though "chai" means "tea." Kelly was always indignant about stuff like that. But despite the cultural mistakes, Harper still loved the film.

Without knowing what to do, she decided to channel Shifu. She closed her eyes and breathed in and out, steady and slow. She filled her lungs and released the air, over and over again until her heartbeat slowed and she could feel the pulsing rhythm coursing through her veins. She began to release the fear and discover a new feeling, one she couldn't name. It came from deep within and felt ancient and powerful. Something beyond her age and her abilities. It frightened her because she knew she was tapping into something elemental and dangerous. It made her aware of how small and insignificant she really was. All her senses were alive and tingling with this awareness.

Was this the spirit realm? Had she entered the world of the dead or was she just more attuned to it? She didn't know the answer, but she felt that something was very different. That she had opened up a channel to another world.

And as she felt this knowledge, she realized she was no longer alone. She opened her eyes to find herself surrounded by curious ghosts.

There were a total of thirty spirits, most wearing clothes from a long time ago. One elderly ghost peered over her round spectacles and shook her head before returning to her ghostly knitting.

"In my day, young children didn't come to cemeteries trying to raise the dead," she tsked. "What is this world coming to?"

"Hooligans! That's what they are!" An old man shook his cane in Harper's direction. "Too much coddling and not enough whupping."

A teenage boy floated around her, examining her. "She must be doing some séance thing," he said. "I'm thinking I might pull her hair real hard or put a spider down her shirt."

Trying to contain her fear, Harper focused on the young girl sitting right in front of her, wearing a pretty white pinafore and knocking her Mary Janes together. Harper could almost hear the ghostly tap of her shoes. She had a slight smile and a bright, curious expression on her young face.

Harper decided she'd start with her. "Please, could you tell your friend not to pull my hair or put a spider down my shirt?"

The little ghost girl's mouth dropped open and there was an excited murmuring from the other ghosts.

"You can see us?" the little girl asked. "Crikey! The only other person who can see us is the little old shaman lady that comes around, but we haven't seen her in a while. Are you a spirit hunter, too?"

Harper shook her head. "What's that?"

"They're special people who hunt down the bad or troubled ghosts and send them on their way to wherever they belong."

"Why doesn't the spirit hunter send all of you on, then?" Harper asked.

"Well, we aren't bothering any humans," the little girl replied.

"Unless they come here." The teenage boy popped up next to the little girl. "Then we might have a wee bit of harmless fun with them, right, Phoebe?" He nudged the little girl, who giggled.

"A spider down my back is harmless fun?" Harper asked in disbelief.

The teenager grinned at her. "What? It's not poisonous."

"The old shaman lady asks us every once in a while if we want to move on, but I'd miss my friends too much," Phoebe said, smiling up at the teenage boy.

"But what about your family?" Harper asked. "Don't you miss them?"

"Yes, but it's been so long since I've seen them, and now everyone here is my family," Phoebe replied.

"Oh," Harper said, not really understanding. She couldn't help but notice that Phoebe looked sad.

"You see, we'd been dead a long time before the spirit hunter showed up," the teenager explained with a shrug. "It would've been different if she'd shown up way earlier."

The old lady with her knitting floated over to sit next to Phoebe.

"Spirit hunters are quite rare," the old lady said with a sigh. "I never saw one for the first fifty years here. Back then, I would've given anything to be with my Gerald again. But we never did have any kids, and now I do. I am content." She smiled at Phoebe, who leaned in for a ghostly embrace.

"Where can I find this spirit hunter?" Harper asked slowly. "She could help me save my brother."

"What's that you say? Speak up! I can't hear you!" the elderly man grumbled.

Harper took a deep breath. "I'm looking for a spiritual adviser. My brother is possessed by the ghost of an evil boy who is haunting my house."

A loud murmuring took over the cemetery as the ghosts all expressed their shock, concern, and curiosity. Harper scrambled to her feet as the ghosts pressed closer. It was a bit overwhelming to feel all of their energies surge up against her so quickly.

"Tell us what happened," the old lady said kindly.

Harper quickly explained and then watched as the ghosts argued among themselves about how best to help her.

"She definitely needs the old shaman lady," said the teenager, whose name was Roderick. "What was her name again? She just told me to call her Grandma."

"Strange," said the old lady, Mrs. Taylor. "I can't remember her name, either."

Harper soon came to realize that ghosts had terrible memories of the living.

"Is there anybody else who might know who she is or how to contact her?" Harper asked.

There was a long silence before someone whispered, "Mrs. Devereux." A palpable shudder went through all the ghosts at the sound of the name.

"Who is Mrs. Devereux?" Harper asked, desperate for information.

"Don't tell her!" the old man shouted, waving his cane again. "We don't want her coming here and scaring all the young 'uns again."

Harper noticed that Phoebe and some of the other young ghosts had disappeared from sight. She turned to Mrs. Taylor.

"Please, ma'am, you must help me before it's too late," she begged. "My brother is in terrible danger."

Mrs. Taylor looked nervous and worried, wringing her hands over her knitting.

"Mrs. Devereux is a spirit. A very old spirit. But the most powerful one we know. When she was alive, she was a dangerous witch and psychic. It's said that she could read a person's thoughts and curse them in the same moment. Now, she visits the dead all over the world, choosing which spirits she will consume to retain her power. They say she prefers the young ones. But last I heard, she was working with the spirit hunter as one of her spirit guides."

Mrs. Devereux sounded terrifying, but if she could help Harper reach the spirit hunter, then she would do whatever it took.

Harper took a deep breath. "Tell me how to reach her."

The old ghost looked around helplessly. "We don't know, dear," she said. "Only another spirit hunter or a medium can contact her."

Despair threatened to overwhelm Harper. "Where can I find one?" she asked.

The little girl ghost reappeared. "Don't you know? You're a medium," she said. "You can reach her yourself."

"Me? But how?"

"The same way you called us," Phoebe said. "But this time, call her by name. Good luck," she whispered before disappearing.

Harper flung herself down on the ground. As she began her breathing exercises, she noticed all the ghosts vanishing until she was alone once again.

This time, she closed her eyes and centered all her thoughts on the name—Mrs. Devereux—with an added plea for help. Over and over again, she chanted the name. In her mind, she envisioned a giant of a ghost with a wicked face that screamed evil. She shuddered even as she focused on the spiritual energy she could feel flowing all around her. The air grew icy cold and then humidly warm, as if she were standing over a New York City subway grate in the wintertime. Harper knew the ghost was there, but was too frightened to open her eyes.

"You certainly have a wild imagination, child," a warm velvety voice chuckled. "I don't think I'm half as frightening as you've imagined me."

Harper opened her eyes to find the form of a beautiful, petite woman standing in front of her. She wore an elegant silk ball gown of coral rose, with a matching head wrap that complemented her dark-brown skin. Harper found herself thinking that if this was Mrs. Devereux, then she didn't look evil at all.

The spirit laughed, a rich sound that was much deeper than her voice.

"Don't be naive, little one. Evil can take all forms," Mrs. Devereux said. Her eyes suddenly looked as if they were lit with fires from deep within her.

Harper scrambled backward until she hit a tree.

The spirit laughed again and languidly waved a delicate fan before her face.

"You look so familiar, little one. Tell me, what is your name."

"Harper Raine."

The spirit looked surprised and then smiled with

what Harper could only describe as wicked delight.

"How delicious," Mrs. Devereux replied. "Wait until I tell Madam about this."

"Is Madam the spirit hunter?" Harper asked eagerly.

"Yes, dearest, and why must you be seeking her?"

"I need her help," Harper said. Quickly she explained what was happening to her brother. The spirit's face grew grave and then stormy.

"This is indeed a dangerous situation," she said. "I will speak to Madam and you will have your answer in the morning."

Harper's relief was so strong she felt tears prick the back of her eyes.

"Thank you so much," she said, her voice gruff with appreciation.

The spirit smiled kindly at her. "Do not worry, my dear. Madam will help your brother. Just go home and wait to hear from her."

Harper nodded, swiping at the tears that leaked from the corners of her eyes.

"I don't know why the other ghosts said all those horrible things about you," she said. "You're not evil at all."

Mrs. Devereux snorted. "When you saw all the ghosts here, did you notice any who looked like me?"

Harper shook her head. She hadn't realized it before.

"That is the real reason they fear me. Some things never change, even in death. This was always a segregated cemetery. No African-Americans are buried here. Next time come find me in Woodlawn Cemetery instead. I assure you the experience will be completely different."

HARPER'S STUPID DC JOURNAL

Entry #18

THE SPIRIT HUNTER

Day 10–Wednesday morning

Harper was up early and anxiously waiting for the spirit hunter to arrive. Luckily she'd been able to sneak back into the house last night without being caught by anyone. Now that she had her full memory back, she could begin to feel the spiritual energy radiating from specific parts of the house. Michael's room, the attic, and the basement were the strongest. They had to be the ghost boy's territory.

At breakfast, Kelly had come out of her room before noon for once and was animatedly talking to their mom about shopping that day. Harper snorted. That would explain why she was already awake. Harper glanced at Michael and noticed the hostile and intent expression on his face as he stared at Kelly. After the mouse incident, Yuna was being extra attentive and affectionate toward Kelly, and Michael was jealous. Or rather, Harper realized, the awful ghost boy was.

Rose had wondered why William hadn't attacked Harper more. It seemed strange, especially after the holy water incident. But Kelly was probably the reason. Harper wondered if she should warn Kelly to be careful. But as she looked at her sister, she realized Kelly would never believe her.

Kelly caught her eye and let out a deep breath. "Hey doughnut cannibal, I'm sorry for losing it on you. I was really upset and didn't know what I was saying. I know you couldn't have put that mouse on my bed. I tell you what, I'll make it up to you later, okay?"

Shocked, Harper could only blink in astonishment. "Okay," she said.

Kelly smiled. "So we're cool, right?"

Harper nodded vigorously.

"Good," Kelly said. "Let's go, Mom!"

"Just a minute," Yuna replied as she searched for something in her purse.

"I wanna come," Michael said loudly.

"No, you don't," Kelly said, giving Michael's hair

a tousle. "You'll be bored."

Michael shoved Kelly's hand away, glaring at her darkly. "I said I wanna come."

Yuna hesitated, which caused Kelly to raise her voice. "What? No, Mom! We won't be able to get any shopping done if he comes."

"She's right," Yuna said to Michael. "It would be best if you stayed home with Harper."

Harper bolted out of the room just as Michael began to scream in rage.

An hour later, Harper's dad came back home from the office to watch Michael, so that Kelly and Yuna could go shopping. Harper stayed put in her room, listening in horrified fascination at the massive temper tantrum that Michael had been throwing the entire time.

As Harper paced the length of her room, wondering when the spirit hunter would show, Rose watched from her perch on the window.

"It's ten thirty already, why isn't she here?" Harper said.

Rose spread her hands helplessly. "Technically she still has an hour and a half to show up before morning's over."

Suddenly, the shrieking ended abruptly and a

minute later the doorbell rang. Harper raced out of her room and down the stairs, just in time to see her father open the door. Instead of the unknown spirit hunter, Harper was surprised and thrilled to hear a familiar well-loved voice.

"Grandma!" Harper shouted as she flew through the foyer and into her grandmother's arms.

"*Omona!* Harper, you grew so big!"

Harper laughed in pure delight. *Omona* was the Korean version of "wow." And it was a word that always reminded her of her grandmother. Grandma Lee was slight and petite and looked far younger than her sixty-plus years. But the best part of her grandmother was her eyes. When Grandma Lee smiled, it started in her eyes.

"Grandma, why haven't you visited us?"

There was a sad smile on Grandma's face. "It's my fault, Harper. I said something that made your mother very unhappy with me. Don't blame her for this." Grandma reached up onto her tiptoes to give Harper's dad a big hug. "Hi, Peter, how are you?"

As the adults began to chitchat, Harper spotted Michael peering around the doorway to the living room, his face expressionless.

"You just missed Yuna and Kelly, but Michael is home," Peter said. Turning, he saw Michael standing in the living room. "Come here, son, and meet your grandmother."

Michael continued to stare for another long moment before turning around and walking away.

"Michael, come back here this instant!"

"That's okay, Peter, let him be," Grandma Lee said, grabbing hold of Harper's hands. "I want to talk to Harper, anyway."

"I don't know what has gotten into him lately," Peter said with an exasperated sigh. "Excuse me while I go have a talk with him."

Harper hugged her grandmother again, so happy to see her. "Do you want to see the house, Grandma?"

Grandma Lee shook her head. "Later. Let's go to your room and chat first."

With a happy nod, Harper led her grandmother up the stairs to her room. When they entered, her grandmother did a curious thing. Before closing the door, she opened her oversized purse and pulled out a ziplock bag filled with what looked like sea salt. She took a handful of salt and tossed it on the ground in front of Harper's door and then closed it. Once inside, she took note of the hanging bells and the empty pouch on the ground. Grabbing the pouch, she reached into her purse again and pulled out a small ziplock bag filled with the same mixture of salt, fennel, and pine needles that was in it before. She stuffed it into the little bag, tied it up, and hung it on the doorknob again.

Grandma Lee then sat on the middle of the floor and took out a brass bowl and a folded piece of white paper. Harper watched in open-mouthed amazement as her grandmother lit the paper on fire and then caught the ball of flames within her hands. She began to chant in Korean until the paper disintegrated into ashes and she dropped them into the bowl. She dusted off her hands and stared at Harper with a grim expression.

"Mrs. Devereux told me you needed my help," she said. "We have no time to lose. Your brother is in grave danger."

HARPER'S STUPID DC JOURNAL

Entry #19

Things I hate:

1. *Not seeing my grandmother for five years*
2. *Michael's first time meeting Grandma ruined by a nasty ghost*

I've missed Grandma Lee so much. I'm so happy to see her again. But I'm also relieved that she is the answer to all our problems. She can save Michael! If only she'd come to the house when we moved in. She probably would have exorcised William before anything bad could have happened to Michael.

Thinking about this makes me mad at my mom for not working things out with Grandma. But now I remember that Mom had a big fight with Grandma and told her not to fill my head with nonsense. And that's when they stopped talking. It was soon after that my grandma stopped coming to see us. I guess Kelly was right after all. It was my fault that Grandma stopped visiting.

SHAMAN

Day 10—Wednesday noon

Harper could feel her mouth gaping open. She couldn't quite grasp the concept that her grandmother was the person she was seeking.

"But I don't understand! How can you be the spirit hunter?" Harper asked.

"I am a *mudang*, a shaman," Grandma Lee said. "This is what I do."

"How come I never knew?"

"Your mom never approved of it. She is too logical. To her it is all mumbo jumbo and impossibilities. She believes only what she can see, and that is a shame." Grandma Lee sighed. "And you can tell your friend to stop hiding. I can feel her hovering around me."

Rose appeared at Harper's side. "You can feel me?"

Grandma Lee smiled. "There you are, my dear—what a lovely ghost! And where have you been all these years?"

"The foyer mirror," Rose replied shyly.

"Ah, but of course!" Grandma Lee said. "I had sensed you before, but I never saw you. I tried to look for you a few times, but Harper's mother doesn't like me to use my tools around the children. Since I knew you were a gentle thing that would never harm my family, I left you alone."

She looked from Rose to Harper and smiled. "And I'm glad I did. I can see you've been a good friend to my granddaughter."

"Rose is my best friend," Harper said.

"I'm so glad to meet you, Rose," Grandma Lee said. "Now tell me all about what happened to Michael."

It took nearly an hour to explain everything that had happened. But Grandma Lee became most upset when she found out about the fire and Harper's hospitalization. She was shocked that no one had told her about what had happened and that Yuna had told Harper not to talk about it with her.

"Foolish girl, if only she had come to me," she said, as her voice filled with pain. "My poor child, what you've suffered because of the stubbornness of your mother . . . I'm so sorry."

Harper could feel the tears pushing up and overflowing. "Oh Grandma! I wish I'd known about you earlier. I've felt like such a freak all my life."

"Freak? Huh, if you are a freak, then so am I!"

She leaned over to hug Harper hard.

"My little girl, there's nothing wrong with you," Grandma Lee said. "People reject things they don't understand. The problem is with them, not with you!"

"Does Mom hate us for being different?"

Grandma Lee sighed. "She doesn't hate us, she hates what we represent. The spirit world is something she refuses to accept. But this time she has no choice. We must save Michael from this ghost child before it is too late."

"What will happen to him, Grandma?"

Her grandmother's face looked so stern that it frightened her.

"If we don't exorcise the ghost child and send it out of the mortal realm, Michael will be lost forever."

"And you can do that?" Harper asked hopefully.

Grandma Lee rose to her feet. "Now that I know exactly what I'm dealing with, I know what I need. Let me gather my tools and I'll be back in an hour. Best to do this while your mom is not home."

Harper nodded. "She won't understand. But what should I do in the meantime?"

"Watch your brother," Grandma Lee said. "Keep track of how different he is acting and behaving. While I could sense that the possession is strong, your brother is still there. He still has the strength to fight it. We will save him."

They went downstairs, where Grandma Lee gave Peter another hug and explained that she'd forgotten something at home and would be back soon.

Harper's dad looked uncomfortable as her grandmother left. He turned to her with a sigh.

"I really want your mom and your grandmother to make their peace," he said. "But I'm worried that this is not a good time, what with all the stress your mother's been under."

"It'll be okay," Harper said. "Mom won't be back until later. You know how Kelly is when she's shopping."

Peter laughed and gave Harper an affectionate hug.

Harper ran back to her room to wait for her grandmother's return. Even though she was afraid for her brother, she was also deeply relieved to know that her grandmother could save him. She was still anxious and afraid, but she no longer felt helpless.

That is, until an eerie sensation crept up Harper's spine. She turned to see Michael standing in her doorway. She hadn't even heard the door open.

Michael cocked his head to the side in a strange, unnatural manner. "Is that old lady coming back?"

"That old lady is our grandma," Harper said sharply. "And yes, she is coming back."

"I don't like her," he said flatly.

Anger surged through Harper hot and strong. The real Michael would have adored seeing his grandmother. A painful ache in her chest made her catch her breath. She missed her real brother and she desperately wanted him back.

"You should be nice to Grandma Lee—she wants to get to know you," she said.

Without acknowledging her, the false Michael stormed off.

Before she could call for Rose, Harper heard the front door open and voices from downstairs. She raced to the foyer and was dismayed to see Kelly and her mom returning from shopping.

"What are you doing back so early?" she asked.

"Food for you guys," Kelly said as she bolted up the stairs with her bags.

Behind her, Yuna held up a big plastic bag that said "Popeyes."

"We thought we'd bring home some lunch for everyone. It's not KFC, but I hear Popeyes' chicken is the best."

Her dad appeared out of nowhere, making a beeline for the bag. "Mmmmmm, I could smell the fried chicken as soon as you walked in the door."

Then fake Michael ran in and threw himself into Yuna's arms. "Mom, you're home! Take me out now!"

Yuna picked him up but shook her head. "We only stopped by to drop off the food. We're heading right back out."

Harper heaved a sigh of relief. Maybe they would leave before Grandma Lee showed up.

"No, don't go out without me! I won't let you!" Michael screamed as Kelly came racing down the stairs.

"Ugh, not again," she said as Michael began to throw a fit. "Come on, Mom, just leave him."

Peter came out of the dining room and tried to grab Michael, but the boy's grip on Yuna's neck was tight and he refused to let go.

"Young man, I'm getting really tired of your nonsense!" Peter said as he tried to pry Michael's hands off.

Kelly opened the front door and stood in the entranceway urging her mom to hurry. In the midst of all the drama, Grandma Lee appeared at the doorway dressed in her full garb of a Korean shaman.

The screaming immediately stopped as fake Michael glared at Grandma Lee, a mixture of fear and hate taking over his face.

"Grandma!" Kelly said in surprise. She squealed in delight as she reached over to give her a quick hug. "It's so good to see you! But I didn't know you were coming. And why are you dressed like that?"

Yuna and Peter both turned to stare in astonishment. Grandma Lee's outfit was a bright-red *hanbok* over layers of white and blue petticoats. Around her waist she wore a colorful belt with bells and an ornamental sheathed sword hanging on one side and a miniature-sized brass gong on the other. On her head, she wore an intricately patterned hat with small bells hanging over her ears. In her arms she carried a small Korean drum and a black bag. As she stepped into the house, the bells rang musically, causing Michael to shriek and cover his ears in pain.

He scrambled out of Peter and Yuna's arms and ran from the room, shouting "Don't let her get me!"

"Mom, what are you doing here?" Yuna's voice was surprised but cold.

"That's not a very polite way to greet your

mother," Grandma Lee responded.

"I would have been happier to see you if you weren't dressed in this ridiculous clothing that scared my child."

"Ridiculous? How can you say that about your heritage? You can reject it as much as you want, but your face cannot hide who you are. You are Korean and you shouldn't be ashamed of it."

"I'm not ashamed of being Korean, I'm ashamed of being your daughter!"

Kelly gasped in shock. Harper was so angry she shouted, "Mom, how could you?" just as her dad said, "Yuna, I think you've gone too far."

Her grandmother, who had stood so bold and proud at first, seemed to wilt and wither.

"I am sorry that you cannot understand what it is I do."

"Do? What do you do? Fool people into believing that ghosts exist. Pretend you are some psychic that can tell fortunes . . ."

"That is not true! I am a *mudang*! I protect people—"

"You protect people! People need protection from you! You pretend to help them in their grief and claim you can contact their loved ones. It's all a lie."

Grandma Lee came forward, reaching a hand out

to her daughter. “Yuna, if this is about your father, I know how badly you wanted to talk to him one last time. I know you wanted to say you were sorry, but there was no reaching out to him because he had moved on. And he knew, he always knew, you loved him. You didn’t need to tell him. He knew.”

Yuna tore her arm away and wheeled back in a fury.

“Don’t talk about my father! Don’t ever talk to me about my father!” Yuna shouted. She turned away for a second. “Look, I just can’t see you right now, Mom. I’m not ready. I thought I was but I’m not. I’m so sorry. Please leave.”

“No!” Harper said. “Grandma has to stay. She has to save Michael; he’s in danger.”

Yuna looked stunned.

“How dare you fill Harper’s head with your lies! I told you before that I wouldn’t let you do that to her. You have to go!”

This couldn’t be happening, Harper thought. The scene before her was too much. Kelly stood frozen by the open door while her father looked too shocked to do anything. Grandma Lee helplessly turned to leave. From the corner of her eye, Harper spotted fake Michael grinning from the kitchen doorway.

“Grandma, I’m going with you!”

Harper ran out the door and held on to her grandmother's arm.

"Harper, get back in here!" Yuna demanded, grabbing hold of the door.

Harper whirled around to face her.

"I'm just like Grandma," Harper said. "And if you can't understand her, then you'll never understand me."

She turned and led her sad grandmother toward the car. "Grandma, we don't have time to worry about Mom. We have to figure out how to help Michael."

Grandma Lee nodded and quickly got into her car. Harper hopped in and put on her seat belt as her mother and father both came out of the house.

"Harper!" they both yelled. But Grandma Lee pulled out of the driveway and drove away.

"I knew your mother was angry with me, but I never realized how deep it went," Grandma Lee muttered.

"You said it was because of Grandpa," Harper said. "What happened?"

It was quiet in the car as Grandma Lee focused on driving. Her face looked so sad.

"You never knew your grandpa, but he was a wonderful man," she said. "Your mother was very close to him. He doted on her so much. But when Yuna was in high school, she was very headstrong, just like her father. One day they had a big fight and she ran off. Her father went out looking for her and he was hit by a drunk driver and killed. Yuna had gone over to her friend's house to cool off. By the time she came home, he was gone. She begged me over and over to let her talk to his spirit. So she could apologize. But his spirit did not linger. There was no reason. He was at peace. I told this to her, but she never believed me. Instead, she decided that there was no such thing as ghosts and that I was a fake."

"That's not fair! She's blaming you for her own mistake!"

Grandma Lee sighed. "You have to be compassionate, Harper. Yuna was only sixteen. In her mind, if ghosts were real, then she couldn't understand why her father wouldn't want to see her one last time. It was easier to think that there were no ghosts than to think that her beloved father would leave without saying good-bye."

A niggling sense of sympathy arose in Harper. She realized that this explained so much about why her mother was the way she was.

"But that happened so long ago. What did you fight about five years ago?"

The car stopped at a red light and Grandma Lee

reached over to pat Harper's hand. "Do you remember when you were seven years old and got very ill?"

"I think so," Harper said. "Dad said I had a bad case of the flu."

The light changed to green and Grandma Lee began driving again. "It wasn't the flu," she said. "It was a malevolent spirit."

Harper gasped. "But how?"

"Your mother loves antiques," Grandma said. "I've always warned her that she has to be careful about what she brings home. Spirits and demons will attach themselves to objects that are meaningful to them, like your friend Rose and her mirror. You know in the old days, they would cover mirrors with blankets to keep ghosts from being trapped."

"But Rose is not malevo—what you said." Harper was indignant.

"Yes, I know. She is lovely and sweet. But the spirit attached to the jewelry box your mom had acquired was evil," Grandma Lee said. "And it made you very sick."

"What happened?"

Grandma Lee was quiet for a few minutes as she navigated the car through the busy streets. "Your mother didn't believe me. She said you had the flu. But I knew why you weren't getting better. At first,

I tried to take the box from your home. But that didn't work. The spirit had already latched on to you, absorbing your energy and your aura. I had no choice but to perform an exorcism. It should've been an easy one except I underestimated the power of the spirit."

As her grandmother spoke, Harper could visualize what happened. She was in bed and she was crying.

"I remember, it was hurting me," she said.

"Yes, during the exorcism, it made you scratch your own face and bang your head on the wall. When I finally exorcised it, you were a bruised and bleeding mess. Your mom was understandably upset. When she asked you what happened, you told her that I got rid of the ghost who was hurting you."

The memory came back with a jolt. Her mother yelling at her grandmother, accusing her of filling her head with nonsense. Now Harper knew what that meant.

"She was so mad . . . ," Harper said.

Grandma sighed. "It's because she doesn't understand."

There was a long silence as both Harper and Grandma Lee were lost in their mutual thoughts.

"I know why Mom was so upset, but it doesn't

mean I forgive her for keeping you from us. She kept you away from us for five years! I missed you so much," Harper said.

"I missed you, too," Grandma said.

"And I will never forgive Mom if we can't save Michael."

"Yes, you're right, we have to focus on your brother now," her grandmother said, driving on.

Fifteen minutes later, they pulled in front of a small Cape Cod–style house.

"So are we in Maryland?" Harper asked.

Grandma Lee nodded. "Rockville. Your mother always liked to tell people she was from Washington, D.C., but technically she is a Marylander."

"How come we never visited you? Why did Mom always make you come see us?"

Her grandmother shrugged. "It was no big deal, really. I travel a lot for my work, anyway. And since your aunt Youjin was in New Jersey, it was easy enough to visit you both."

They got out of the car and hurried up to the door. "But the real reason she didn't want any of you to visit is what is inside."

She unlocked the door and entered the house. Immediately, Harper was hit by the strong odor of incense and citrus. As they took their shoes off at the entranceway, a little dog with black and golden-brown hair came running over, his tail wagging furiously.

"Monty!" Harper plopped down onto the floor and let the little dog jump right into her lap and lick her all over her face.

"He remembers you," Grandma Lee said. "Come, Monty, leave her alone."

Monty jumped off Harper's lap and went immediately to Grandma Lee's side.

In the living area, there was a beige sofa and love seat and a long antique-looking coffee table with several drawers on each side. Over the sofa there was an old family photo of her grandma and grandpa with two young girls. Harper almost didn't recognize them as her mother and aunt. On the other wall, there hung a cross over a table with more family photos. There was nothing out of the ordinary about the space, although Harper was surprised by the gigantic flat-screen television. It was larger than the one in her house.

Grandma Lee noticed her surprise and smiled. "That was a present from a grateful client," she said. "Now I get to watch my Korean dramas in high definition."

"Client?" Harper asked. "How much do you get paid for your work?"

Grandma Lee put down her bags on the dining table and walked into the kitchen. "I never ask for money," she said. "They give me what they can afford. Sometimes it is money and sometimes it is other things."

She rummaged through the refrigerator and returned with a bowl of bright orange persimmons. "Eat. You need the energy for what you are about to do."

"Me?" Harper asked. "What am I going to do? You're the one who has to save him."

Grandma Lee peeled another persimmon and began to eat it. "Your mother will never let me in now to do what's necessary. It is up to you. I will teach you."

Harper absentmindedly put a piece of the persimmon in her mouth. She was surprised at how sweet and delicious it was. Monty sat at her feet, looking up at her with his tongue hanging out.

"How can I do anything? I'm just a kid!"

"Did you forget that you can see and speak to spirits? That is a great power. And I will teach you how to use your power to vanquish this ghost. Now come with me."

Harper quickly finished off the rest of her snack and followed her grandmother down the narrow hallway. Monty whined as he stayed at the edge of the hallway.

"Why isn't Monty coming?" Harper asked.

"He doesn't like this room very much," her grandmother said.

They went inside a small room and entered what looked like another world.

Inside was a shrine. Her grandmother knelt before a large and elaborate altar. She lit several incense sticks, placed them in an urn, and began to chant. On the altar table there were large brass bowls of oranges, apples, bottles of rum, and even a bowl filled with candy. The altar also held a large open fan, a brass drum and drumstick, cymbals, and several vases of flowers. Behind the table, the wall was covered with colorful paintings of ancient people. Lining both sides of the altar were various Korean costumes hanging from the walls. A child's *hanbok* as well as one that could be worn by royalty hung on the right side while two male *hanboks* were showcased on the left. On the floor before the altar stood a large *janggu*, a double-headed hourglass-shaped drum.

Harper was staring at the paintings when she felt a presence materialize next to her.

"Those are the ancient gods of Korea, although I'm sure this painting doesn't do them justice," a velvety voice said. "The mountain deity San-shin, the ocean deity Bada-shin, and Princess Bari, the first *mudang.* Whoever painted them wasn't very good, were they. I can't imagine they really all have the same face and jowly cheeks. If Father Rios at your grandmother's church knew about this room, he'd have her excommunicated so fast."

Harper turned to see Mrs. Devereux floating next to her.

"Now now, don't tease her, my dear. She's been through enough already," Grandma Lee said with an affectionate smile. "I know that you two have already met."

"It is a great pleasure to meet Madam's talented granddaughter," Mrs. Devereux said with a graceful incline of her head. "After all these years, it is good to see that you've finally found an apprentice, and in your own family, too."

"Not just one," Grandma Lee said. "Michael has it, too, which is why the possession is so strong."

"But we can save him, you said." Harper was too anxious to focus on anything but her brother.

"Yes, that is why I summoned Mrs. Devereux," she said. "Your mother might stop me from entering your house, but she can't stop Mrs. Devereux."

The spirit smiled at Harper in a way that did not reassure her at all.

"I don't mean to be rude, Grandma, but what does Mrs. Devereux do for you?"

"She is my spirit guide. Has been for nearly forty years. One of the best there is. I would be lost without her," Grandma Lee said. She was bustling all around the altar, gathering a bunch of things.

"Madam is kind but she is also right. I am one of the most powerful spirit allies she has and I will make sure to help you and your brother."

This time Harper was reassured by the kindness she saw in the spirit's face. Mrs. Devereux was an intimidating ghost, but Harper instinctively knew she would not hurt her.

Having collected everything she needed, Grandma Lee sat in front of Harper again with Mrs. Devereux drifting into a seated position next to her.

Grandma Lee spread out a multicolored Korean scarf and set out three brass bowls, two short-handled bells, and what looked like fancy jingle bells, the kind you see in school music classrooms. The long metal handle split into two dragon heads, each of which held a ring of six tiger bells in its mouth. Next to this, she placed a stack of neatly folded, crisp white paper, a lighter, a large container of sea salt, and a plastic bottle filled with what looked like water.

"Harper, in order to drive the evil spirit from your brother's body, you must use all of these tools," her grandmother said. She picked up the jingle bells first. "These are *mudang* bells, the tools of every Korean *mudang*. They summon the spirits to you. You must be careful to name the spirit you are calling, otherwise, with your powers, you could become quickly overwhelmed by the dead. You must not use these bells until you are ready to release the spirit from Michael's body."

Harper shuddered at her words, but Grandma Lee didn't notice. She placed the three bowls in front of her next.

"These are your purification bowls. They are used to trap the spirit," she said. She took a piece of paper and lit it over the middle bowl, cupping the burning paper in her hands and then dropping the ashes into the bowl.

She grabbed the water bottle and poured it into the other two bowls. "This is holy water blessed by the priests at St. Elizabeth's."

"You're using Catholic holy water in a shaman ritual?"

"This is not a shaman ritual," her grandmother said. "This is an exorcism of an evil spirit. It crosses the boundaries of all religions, and we must use the power of all rituals of good to defeat it."

Grandma Lee then placed the short-handled bells next to the two bowls filled with holy water.

"These bells are based on Buddhist principles of wisdom and truth." She rang each one once. "Wisdom" had a bright medium sound that was crystal clear. "Truth" sounded lower and deeper in tone.

"Wisdom opens the spiritual pathways, for knowledge is power. Truth reveals what is hidden, for a spirit cannot hide from the sound of truth.

"The sound of these bells is anathema to an evil spirit—it will immobilize them when used with the proper words. When you ring the bell of Wisdom you must say, 'Through the power of the Ancient One, I bind you. You will do no harm.' When you ring the bell of Truth you must say, 'Through the power of the Worthy One, I bind you. You will do no harm.' And you must repeat these chants over and over until the spirit is weak. If he is possessing Michael, you must use your *mudang* bells to force him out. And, once he's out, you must say, 'Leave this world. Return to the land of the dead. I release you!' Only then will he be defeated."

"But how will I know when he is weak?" Harper could hear how shrill her voice sounded. The creeping fear that had been rising within her ever since her grandmother had told her she would have to exorcise the ghost threatened to send her into panic.

Mrs. Devereux shimmered beside her. "Don't worry, little spirit hunter, you will know when the time is right."

Some of her panic subsided at the words, but still the fear remained. She stared at the items that her grandmother was now carefully packing into a bag.

"What about the salt?" she asked. "What is that for?"

"Oh my goodness! How could I forget! Before you do anything, you must form a circle of salt around yourself to protect you from the spirit."

"Salt will protect me?"

"It is one of the purest substances in the world. Evil cannot abide it."

Harper nodded. "Do I need to wear a *hanbok* like you do, Grandma?"

The spirit guide laughed and even Grandma Lee

smiled. "No, my dear. This is my way. It is steeped in the culture of the Korean *mudang*. But you are not a *mudang* or a shaman. You are a young spirit hunter in a new country. And you must find your own way."

"But these things you are giving me, they'll work for me even if I'm not a *mudang*?"

Mrs. Devereux floated up in front of her. "These instruments in another person's hands would be meaningless," she said. "They have no power alone. But in the hands of a powerful spirit hunter, they become dangerous weapons. You have that ability."

"But how do you know that?"

"Because I felt your power," Mrs. Devereux said. "You summoned an entire cemetery of ghosts. You willed them to help you, and then you summoned me. That is the act of a powerful spirit hunter. You must channel your spiritual energy, the pure force within you that allows you to see us. And when you face this spirit, if you find yourself in need of me, I will be near."

Grandma Lee urged Harper out of the shrine room and down the hallway. Monty barked and twirled happily to see them.

"You must go now," she said. "Everything you need is here. Once you get home, choose a spot where you will not be disturbed by your family and begin the purification ritual. Then summon Mrs. Devereux. You don't want her to come too early or you will lose the element of surprise. She will help you in my stead. Quickly, put your shoes on."

"Grandma, how'm I supposed to go without you?" she said, panicked.

Just then the doorbell rang. Monty barked and hid behind Harper.

Grandma Lee opened the door. Harper's father stood at the doorstep.

"It took you a while to get here," she said. "Did you get lost?"

He looked sheepish. "My GPS went a little wonky and took me the long way here. I have no idea what's wrong with it."

Grandma Lee looked up at Harper and winked. "Strange how that happened," she said.

"I'm sorry about Yuna," he said. "She's been under a lot of stress lately."

"No need to apologize to me, Peter," Grandma said. "I know my daughter very well. I understand. You go on and take Harper home now."

After hugging her grandmother tight and giving Monty a last kiss good-bye, Harper held her bag close to her chest and ran past her dad to the car. Peter got into the car and programmed his GPS.

"Hopefully we won't have any problems going home," he said.

"Don't worry, we won't," Harper said knowingly.

HARPER'S STUPID DC JOURNAL

Entry #20

Things I hate:

1. *Being afraid*

THE BATTLE FOR MICHAEL

Day 10–Wednesday afternoon

When they returned home, absolute chaos awaited them. Kelly was in hysterics. She had a large gash on her forehead, which was bleeding badly, along with a bloody nose.

"What happened?" Peter yelled as he rushed to help quell the blood.

"Michael went ballistic when Kelly said we were going shopping again," Yuna said. "He smashed his fire truck into Kelly's face and ran away. He's hiding somewhere in the house now. I was just about to call an ambulance."

"It'll be faster if I drive," Peter said. "You stay home and find Michael."

"No!" Kelly sobbed as she clutched her mother's arm. "Mom has to come, too!"

Harper pushed her dad toward the door. "Go, Dad, I'll be all right."

"But what if he attacks you, too?"

Harper shook her head. "He might have surprised Kelly, but I'll be on the lookout. And he's still only four years old."

"Peter, we have to go," Yuna said as she guided Kelly to the door. Before they left, Kelly turned to Harper.

"Be careful. There really is something wrong with Michael," she said in tears.

She stepped out before Harper could respond.

"I'm just going to drop them off and come right back," Peter said. "I'll be less than an hour. Keep an eye out for him but leave him alone."

He gave Harper a quick hug and took off. As Harper stood at the window, watching them drive away, Rose appeared by her side.

"He's in his room," she whispered. "And he knows why you're here."

As Rose spoke, the walls began to ooze a thick

black liquid and the lights in the room flickered on and off in rapid succession. Rose moved closer to Harper, and Harper wished her friend was flesh and blood. She could have used the comfort of a solid hug.

"He's trying to scare you," Rose said. "What did your grandmother say to do?"

"She gave me bells . . . ," Harper whispered, too scared to explain further.

"Okay, I don't know what that means, but you might want to use them . . . now," Rose said.

Harper gulped and proceeded up the stairs, careful not to touch the oozing, pulsing slime that threatened them.

"Rose, you're a ghost. You shouldn't be afraid of other spirits," Harper exclaimed. "They can't technically hurt you."

"We don't know that for sure," Rose said. "This ghost is really evil."

"Stop saying that," Harper said. "I'm scared to death as it is."

"Sorry."

A sudden unholy shriek pierced their ears and a blast of wind sent Harper's hair flying every which way. The temperature in the hall dropped so low, Harper's breath blew frosty before her.

She reached the bend in the stairway and turned.

With a frightened scream, Rose disappeared. Harper wished she could, too. Her mouth dropped open, but she was too scared to scream. Standing on the step above her was the large maggot-ridden body of a decaying corpse. Half of its face had rotted to the bone while the other half was covered in grayish-green peeling skin.

Was now the right time to summon Mrs. Devereux? Was this when her need was greatest?

Harper stared in frozen terror as the corpse stretched its decomposing hands toward her neck.

Rose shouted, "Quick, Harper! Use the bells your grandmother gave you!"

Shaken, Harper grabbed for a bell from her bag so quickly she didn't even know which one it was. She pulled it out and rang it hard in front of the corpse's face. At the loud toll of the bell, the corpse exploded into nothingness. Harper had grabbed Wisdom. With her heart pounding in her ears and her chest tight with fear, she rang the bell with each step she took, causing the coldness to recede a little more. By the time she reached the top of the stairs, she was ringing the bell to a steady rhythm. Turning to face the coldest room in the house, she let the bell fall silent and stared in horror at what was happening around her.

The hallway seemed to elongate before her eyes and the walls began to bleed. From the dripping red walls, pale skeletal arms extended themselves outward, trying to reach for her. A loud, ugly voice bellowed, "Go away! You're not welcome here. If you come any closer, I'll kill you!" It sounded like William's voice but older and scarier.

Harper's body was at war with her heart. Everything inside her begged her to run away, but the memory of her brother, her real brother, compelled her to stay. She could see him giggling and calling out "Catch me, Harper!" as he ran around in a big goofy circle, making it easy for her to grab him in her arms. She remembered when she'd come back from the hospital after Briarly, all wrapped up in bandages and casts. Michael had wrapped his arm in toilet paper, like a mummy, to sympathize with her pain. He'd gotten into bed with her and comforted her. She could see his sweet face swooping in for a wet, messy kiss, saying "I love you best" in his husky little-boy voice.

"No," she shouted. "I want my brother back!"

She stepped forward and rang her bell loudly.

The house shook and a hurricane-like wind blew through the hallway, sending the picture frames flying off the walls. A large bureau came crashing out of the master bedroom toward her.

"Watch out!" Rose yelled. She materialized and pulled Harper out of the way just as the heavy bureau smashed into the wall behind them.

Harper rang the bell harder and shouted into the wind. "You can't have him! Michael, I'm coming for you!"

She was almost to Michael's room. The bloody skeleton arms snatched at Harper's hair, trying to stop her. A bright sliver of light pulsed from under the closed door. She went to grab the doorknob, but it morphed into the head of a large snake, which lunged at Harper's hand. Harper dropped her bell and bag, falling back. Immediately hands pulled at her hair, her clothing, her skin, trying to drag her into the wall. Desperate, she fought against the arms, trying to reach for her bell, but it was too far away.

"Rose, help me!"

Rose instantly appeared and pushed the bell into Harper's outstretched fingers. Harper grabbed the handle and rang the bell fiercely. In a loud, commanding voice, she shouted, "Release me!"

The hands melted away and Harper and Rose were alone in the hallway.

"Thank you," Harper said. "But stay hidden until I call you."

Rose nodded once, full of determination, before she faded away.

Harper pushed herself up, groaning at the ache in her muscles and the soreness of her arm where her stitches were. It was surprising how painful fright could be. The doorknob was now normal again, but the strange light still pulsed from beneath the doorframe.

"Michael, I'm coming for you," Harper whispered. Gripping the doorknob, she turned it and entered.

In the middle of the room stood the ghostly figure of the vengeful boy. He looked the same as he did in her visions, except for his eyes, which were almost all black and gleamed with a malevolent intensity. Harper took a swift scan of the room and saw Michael fast asleep on his bed.

"It's not fair," William said. "Mother always loved him more!"

Harper knelt on the ground and placed her bag in front of her. Surreptitiously, she pulled the bowls and the bells out and placed them on the floor, in the shadow of her bag.

"Do you mean your brother, Jonathan? I don't think she loved him more," Harper said. "I just think she was worried about him, because he was always getting hurt." By you, she thought. "But mothers don't love one kid more than the other."

William's face changed as he gave her a sly smile. "Your mom loves Kelly more than you," he said. "Anyone can see that. She doesn't like you at all."

Harper paused and closed her eyes. "That's not a very nice thing to say," she said. She took out her bottle of holy water, the lighter, and the paper, and hid them under her bag. "But is that why you hurt Kelly? Because you think my mom loves her best?"

"I hate her! She was stealing my mommy!" William shouted.

The room darkened.

"But she's not your mommy, William. She's mine," Harper said. "Your mom and brother died a long time ago."

The lights flickered and the whole house began to shudder.

"You're just like the rest! You want to take my mother away! But I won't let you!"

Harper was finally ready. Now was the time to call forth the spirit guide. It had to be.

"Mrs. Devereux, I summon you!" Harper shouted.

The air turned electric, and a warm wind filled the room.

"At your service, dearest," Mrs. Devereux said as she materialized in the room.

The ghost boy snarled in fury.

Mrs. Devereux floated next to Harper, still staring down William, even as she urged Harper to start the ritual.

"There's something peculiar about this spirit," she muttered. "Quick! Begin the purification procedure!"

With trembling fingers, Harper lit the white paper and let it burn over the empty bowl in front of her.

"Girl child! You forgot to ring the salt!" Mrs. Devereux cried out.

Harper gasped and reached for the salt container, but William had vanished. Suddenly cold fingers wrapped tightly around Harper's neck, trying to crush her vocal cords.

"Harper, he's behind you!" Rose yelled. "Get away from her, you little monster!"

Rose's incorporeal form rushed at William, sending them both hurtling through the air.

With the pressure off her neck, Harper immediately completed the salt circle and began chanting and ringing the bells.

"Through the power of the Ancient One, I bind

you. You will do no harm. Through the power of the Worthy One, I bind you. You will do no harm."

Harper swung her bells hard as she repeated the chant.

The ghost boy howled, shattering the glass in the windows and sending large pointed shards straight at Harper. She didn't flinch. Her eyes were focused on William. Her every thought was on vanquishing him. The shards embedded in the wall behind her. The room suddenly burst into flames and the temperature skyrocketed.

Harper panicked. Visions of the other fire in the school made her cringe back in fear.

"Don't stop, Harper! The fire is not real!" Mrs. Devereux cried out.

With a deep shuddering breath, Harper straightened up and tightened her grip. Sweat rolled down her face, but still she continued to chant and ring the bells.

On the seventh round, William's form began to fade in and out.

"Stop it! You're hurting me! I want my mommy!"

Harper once again felt the small but strong fingers trying to crush her throat, stopping her chant midway. William remained five feet in front of her, his black eyes large in a pale face contorted with fury. Glancing desperately around her, she realized she'd broken the salt circle with her foot.

"Leave her alone!" Rose yelled as she tried to attack William again. But the vengeful spirit was stronger than her, blasting her out of the room.

Suddenly, the pressure eased and William changed to a regular boy.

"Mommy?" he said, his face appearing innocent and wondering. "Is that really you?"

Harper turned her head painfully and saw the ghostly figure of a woman. She looked exactly like she did in Harper's visions of William's past. But how could that be?

"William, darling!" the new ghost said, holding out her arms.

"Mommy! You came back for me!" William floated happily toward his mother.

The ghost mom looked straight at Harper and yelled, "Now, girl child!" in Mrs. Devereux's voice. Only then did Harper realize who this apparition really was.

William stopped in midair. "Mommy?" His face contorted from happiness to fury. "You're not my mommy!"

Just as William shrieked in rage, Harper rang her bells again. This time she opened up her mind to the spirit realm just like she had back in the cemetery. She focused deeply, tapping into the ancient power as all her senses came into razor-sharp focus.

"Through the power of the Ancient One, I bind you. You will do no harm. Through the power of the Worthy One, I bind you. You will do no harm."

The words now were infused with the power that Harper was channeling from the spirit realm. A lamp came flying across the room at Harper's head. Mrs. Devereux batted it out of the air as if it were a fly.

"Keep chanting, Harper, it's working," she urged.

A small fire erupted around Harper again, but it was nowhere near as powerful as the first. In the air above her, William's form morphed and twisted as he fought against Harper's control. Harper ignored it all and continued to chant. The ghost boy's howls grew less and less and then faded altogether. Harper looked up to find him frozen in place, his face a hideous mask of anger and fear.

Twice more she repeated the refrain and rang the bells. When she was filled with the knowledge that the time was right, she spoke the final words of the chant. "Leave this world. Return to the land of the dead. I release you!"

There was a loud cracking sound, like a thunderbolt strike nearby, and then an ear-splitting shriek, which made Harper cover her ears. And then William's frozen form splintered and exploded into nothingness just as the water in Harper's bowl turned inky dark and sludgelike.

Harper sagged in relief.

Mrs. Devereux exhaled loudly and returned to her normal state. "You did well, little one," she said. "You must dispose of the residue, it is the evil remains of the ghost boy. You must get rid of it before it attracts bad things."

Harper recoiled in disgust. "What do I do? Flush it down the toilet?"

"No, that won't work," Mrs. Devereux said. "The best place to get rid of it is directly in a large body of running water. A river or the ocean. The next best place is to dispose of it on sacred church grounds."

Before Harper could ask how she was supposed to move this disgusting and toxic substance to the church, she heard someone calling her name.

"Harper?"

It was her little brother's sweet voice.

"Michael! Is that really you?"

"Harper, I feel sick," he said. He slid off the bed and then sat on the floor, holding his head in his hands. "My head hurts, too."

Harper scrambled to her feet.

"Wait, Harper!" Mrs. Devereux shouted.

But Harper couldn't wait. She rushed over to hug her brother.

"Michael, I've been so worried about you!"

Her brother's small arms hugged her tight around her neck and then began to strangle her.

"Back away, foul creature!" Mrs. Devereux shouted, and sent a pulse of energy at Michael.

The stranglehold released as Michael's body was thrown away from Harper. She scrambled back and stared at him in horror. His face was no longer Michael's. It was the face of a very pale, creepy old man. He had a receding hairline and stringy gray hair that hung down to his neck. But his eyes looked like a lizard's. The pupils were red with a black slit running down the middle.

"I know you!" Mrs. Devereux hissed. "Professor Grady! You're the one who tried to control the dead."

"And now I can," he said with an evil grin. His form overtook that of Michael's, so that his elongated shadow extended from Michael's torso in a macabre rendition of a reverse puppet show. With a flick of his hands, and a whispered phrase, he froze Mrs. Devereux in place. Then with another flick, she vanished.

THE CURSE OF GRADY

Day 10—Wednesday afternoon, finale

"What did you do to her?" Harper asked.

"This is my domain. She was an uninvited guest so I sent her away," he said as he turned his shadow form toward her. "And don't bother trying to summon her. I've sealed this house tight."

Harper's panic immediately turned to Rose. Where was she? Was she okay?

"Control the dead? What did she mean by that?" Harper asked. Her eyes darted around the room, looking to see how far she was from her bells and bowls.

"It means just what you think it means," Grady

said with a hideous smile. "I am master of all dead things."

He raised his hands and a horde of large black rats surged out from the walls, stampeding toward Harper. She screamed and covered her eyes. She could hear his old raspy laugh—hoarse from disuse. She wished he'd choke on it.

"I've been stuck in this house for over one hundred years," he continued, floating away from Michael's body, which remained frozen in place. "One stupid mistake and I found myself staring down at my own disintegrating body."

"But the police never found you," Harper said in disgust.

The ghost turned to face her. "That's because they're a bunch of fools and nitwits. They never looked under the basement, did they? I have a secret lab that no one has ever found."

That explained why the basement was so frightening. Harper shuddered to think of Grady's nasty decaying body in her house.

Keep talking, old man, she thought. "What happened? How did you die?" Harper asked as she shifted slowly back.

"I believed I'd figured out the secret to immortality, but it wasn't until I died that I realized the truth," he said, vanishing and reappearing centimeters in front of Harper's face, stopping her in her tracks. "I had to die to become immortal."

His ghost form seemed to become more substantial, lengthening to make him tall and thin. His long graying hair flowed around his shiny bald spot. His small, beady red eyes scowled fiercely at her over a large hooked nose and thin lips.

"Thank you for getting rid of William," Grady continued. "William was very useful to me over the years, becoming friends with the little ones, but he had some serious mommy issues. It was quite annoying, and often got in the way of my own plans. In fact, I was going to get rid of him myself once this body was secured."

"What do you want with my brother?"

The shadow man smiled. "What a stupid question, little girl," he mocked. "What would any dead thing like me want with a young, innocent, living body?"

His smile grew wide and leering as he shrank back down into Michael's form. His old-man voice came from Michael's lips. "To live again, of course. That is the secret to immortality."

"No!" Harper shouted in despair. "You leave him alone!" It was a perversion to see her baby brother's face change into an expression that was old and wicked.

An invisible force gripped her by the neck, lifted her up, and slammed her against the wall. The stranglehold grew tighter and tighter as Harper struggled to breathe. She tried to break free of the force that held her in place. With her mind, she frantically called for help, hoping that Rose was still in the house.

Just then the door to the bedroom banged open and Rose appeared in the doorway, shrieking like a banshee while she hurled things into the room, bombarding Michael's body. Things like balls, magazines, crayons, and small toys—all things that wouldn't hurt Michael but would break Grady's concentration. It worked, as Harper fell to the ground, gulping for air. She crawled madly toward her bells and saw Rose's form vanish before her. With no time to process what had happened to her best friend, Harper snatched up her bells and rang them hard, chanting the first refrain loudly.

She was knocked flat on her back by Michael, her arms pinned painfully behind her. His small form shouldn't have weighed more than thirty pounds, but he was pressing down on her with the force of hundreds.

"Michael, please," Harper begged.

"You foolish girl." Grady's face and voice overlaid

Michael's. "I have waited over a century to live again. You will not stop me."

Michael's heavy wooden toy chest rose into the air and slowly floated toward Harper's head.

"So many years I have dreamed of the chance to relive my life once again in this marvelous age. But none of the previous boys would do," Grady gloated. "This boy, however, is powerful. His aura is strong. He will serve me well in both the land of the living and the dead."

Tears welled in the corners of Harper's eyes as she searched Michael's transformed face for any hint of her little brother. The toy chest was now right above her head.

"Michael," she whispered. "If you can hear me, please fight. Don't give up. Don't let him win. I love you."

In that moment, she saw a flicker in her brother's face as his body went slack.

And then she heard her real brother's voice. "Harper, move!"

Harper whirled from under her little brother's body just as the toy chest crashed down right where her head had been. She threw her body toward her bag and dove for the salt container, but she felt strong ghostly hands grip her ankles tight and drag her back.

"This vessel is mine! You can't stop me!"

Harper felt her body being lifted in the air as a shock of electricity coursed through her, so painful she couldn't help but scream.

"Ah, the power of the incorporeal form," Grady said. "So much raw energy, but no life force. Just imagine what I will be able to do with this body once it is grown! I will be the most powerful being in the world. And I will be immortal! But you, sadly, are not."

Grady sent another burst of lightning through Harper. The pain was intense and Harper didn't think she could withstand it for another second when it suddenly stopped and she fell to the ground. Her brother's body stood covering his face while Grady's voice screamed in pain. Shocked, she looked around to see a frightened Dayo holding a large container of salt. Dayo rushed over and dumped the salt in a big wide circle around them.

"Dayo!" Harper couldn't believe her friend was there. "How'd you get here?"

Dayo spun within their circle, adding more salt all around them. "I was walking Pumpkin, and I saw your mom and dad driving away. I could hear your sister crying in the car. I knew something must be really wrong so I ran home to grab some salt."

"How'd you know about the salt?"

"The internet, silly," Dayo said. "Salt is pure and evil can't stand it. And there's definitely something evil in your brother!"

She gasped as Michael uncovered his face to reveal red, burning eyes. Dayo let out a squeak of fear and clutched Harper's arm.

"What do we do now?"

Harper spied her bells and bowls a little ways away from their circle. She grabbed the salt and, extending her arm, shook the salt in a quick circle around her things.

The red-eyed creature stood beyond the salt line, staring malevolently at them. With shaking hands, Harper gathered her things together before her and knelt down on the floor. She dashed aside the ashes from the third bowl and filled it with water. She took hold of her bells and closed her eyes, immediately opening up the channel to the spirit world. Launching into her chant, Harper rang her bells with all her strength. This time, she was more confident in herself and she could hear how her voice rang with power. Inside her mind, she separated the ghost of the old man from her brother. She took a deep breath and in her mind she imagined the binding spell actually working. She visualized the long twisty metal chains that wrapped around and around the ghost. "I bind you, you will do no harm," she chanted over and over again.

"Whatever you're doing is working!" Dayo shouted.

Harper opened her eyes and found Michael's little body frozen before her. Only his eyes looked alive with fear and anger. The binding was complete.

This time Harper reached for the *mudang* bells to force the old ghost out of Michael's body. She stood up and rattled them in front of Michael's face.

"Leave this world. Return to the land of the dead. I release you!"

Grady's voice erupted in fury from Michael's lips. "Never!" His red eyes flickered and turned all white as his body began to twitch.

"Leave this world. Return to the land of the dead. I release you!"

Michael's body convulsed and the spirit flew out of his mouth in a blast of frigid air. Michael collapsed on the ground unconscious, while the spirit hovered in a frozen state above him.

"Leave this world. Return to the land of the dead. I release you!"

This time Harper grabbed up Wisdom and Truth again, rang them hard, and shouted, "Get out of my house!"

The spirit exploded with a loud, echoing shriek, and then faded into nothingness. A second bowl of water turned dark and thick.

Harper threw down her bells and rushed to her brother's side.

"Michael," she cried. She gathered him into her arms and hugged him tight.

"You're squishing me," a little voice whispered.

"Michael, it's you!" Harper shouted. She helped him sit up and then hugged him hard again. This time, he hugged her back.

"Harper, you saved me," Michael said. "I was so scared, but you saved me!"

She blinked back her tears. "You're my baby brother," she said. "I'll always be there for you."

There was the loud bang of the front door and then a familiar voice called Harper's name.

"Grandma?" Harper was amazed. "Grandma! We're up here!"

A short while later, the door opened and their grandmother appeared.

"You're all right," Grandma Lee said with a huge sigh of relief.

She knelt in front of Michael and shook his hand. "I'm your grandma," she said. "I've wanted to meet you for a very long time."

"Hi, Grandma," Michael said shyly.

"But I don't understand," Harper said. "How'd you know it was safe to come?"

"I didn't," Grandma Lee said. "When Mrs. Devereux was pushed out of the house, she sent for me. I drove over as fast as I could, but I see you didn't need me at all!"

"Harper was awesome," Michael chimed in. "She's a great ghost fighter."

"You mean a spirit hunter," said Rose, who suddenly appeared in the doorway.

"Rose! You're safe!" Harper was so relieved. "I didn't know what happened to you."

"Grady only pushed me back into my mirror, not out of the house. But I was trapped until a minute ago," Rose said with a big smile. "Harper, you defeated two evil spirits! You are amazing!"

Harper didn't feel amazing. She felt exhausted and shaky and yet completely exhilarated, too.

Michael was staring in alarm at Rose. He hid his face when Rose smiled at him.

"Michael, this is my best friend Rose and she lives in our foyer mirror," Harper said. "Don't be afraid of her. She will never hurt you."

As Michael greeted Rose, Harper remembered Dayo. She turned around to see her friend curled up into a tight ball, staring at them.

"Grandma, this is my other best friend, Dayo. We're so lucky she came and rescued us!" Harper kneeled by her friend's side. "Dayo! Are you okay?"

Dayo looked at her in a daze. "Who's Rose?" she asked.

With a sigh of relief, Harper gave Dayo a hug.

"Is Rose a ghost?" Dayo whispered into Harper's ear. "Because there's one floating in the air next to your grandmother."

"You can see her?" Harper asked, releasing Dayo in excitement.

"But where'd she go?" Dayo asked, sitting up. "She just disappeared."

"Harper, touch your friend again," Grandma Lee said.

Confused, Harper grabbed Dayo's hand.

Dayo jumped. "She's back!" Dayo said as Rose waved hello. "How are you doing that, Harper?"

Harper shrugged her shoulders. "I have no idea."

The friends looked at each other in amazement. Dayo proceeded to grab and release Harper's hand all the while staring at Rose in amazement.

"It's definitely you," Dayo said, holding tightly to her friend's hand. "I can't see her unless I'm touching you."

Grandma Lee was now kneeling before the three brass bowls, examining them.

"Harper's powers are growing," she said. "She clearly wants you to see Rose, which is why you can see her when she touches you."

Grandma Lee then took out a Tupperware container from her oversized purse and poured the dark sludge-like substance from two of the bowls into it, sealing it tightly afterward. She then gathered all the bowls and the bells and took them into the bathroom.

"What is she doing?" Dayo asked.

Harper shrugged. Her grandmother came back, wiping the bowls and bells dry with a white silk cloth, before packing them all back in their bag, which she then placed in front of Harper.

"Congratulations," Grandma Lee said. "You are now an apprentice spirit hunter."

Harper was surprised. "What does that mean, Grandma?"

"It means that you have the ability to help those people who need protection from lost souls or evil spirits like this one." She raised up the Tupperware container and gave it the stink eye. "There's still much to learn, like how to get rid of this evil spiritual residue. You must—"

"Dump it into a large body of running water or

holy ground like a church cemetery."

Grandma Lee looked impressed. "How did you know that?"

"Mrs. Devereux was explaining it to me before she was cast out," Harper said.

"There's no greater teacher than Mrs. Devereux," Grandma Lee said. She put the container into her purse and then looked around the room at the mess caused by the spirits. "Now I think we'd better clean this place up before your parents get home."

Harper was confused. "Grandma, if the fire wasn't real, then how come all of the rest of it is?"

"Because there's no fire in the room," she said. "They can only manipulate what is here. Anything else is an illusion."

Grandma Lee then turned to Rose and held out a hand. "Rose, will you be a dear and lend me some of your energy?"

The ghost girl looked confused, but she obediently floated over to Grandma Lee and laid her hands over the old woman's outstretched ones. Grandma Lee closed her eyes and the room began to right itself. The heavy toy chest floated back to its corner, crayons and books and all the other things that had been thrown around returned to their proper places. And the messy ring of salt and all the broken glass vanished. The only thing that wasn't fixed was the gaping hole in the window.

Harper, Dayo, and Michael just stared in shock. "How did you do that, Grandma? Is it magic?" Michael asked.

She shook her head and grinned. "It's concentrated energy. I tapped into the spirit realm and used Rose as my conductor. In my youth I could do it all on my own, but now I am old and get too exhausted. So I need a little help."

Harper gasped in excitement. "Does that mean I'll be able to do it also?"

Grandma Lee nodded. "You both will," she said. She reached down and gave Michael a hug. "You are powerful, too, little one."

They heard the sound of the front door opening and closing. Rose disappeared and reappeared.

"It's your mom," she said.

Harper reached out to grab her grandmother's arm. "I won't let her send you out."

"Don't worry, Harper, it will be fine," Grandma Lee said. At that moment, Yuna appeared at the door and stared in surprise at the scene. Grandma Lee sat on the floor, Michael in her lap, with Harper and Dayo standing next to her.

"I see you got my message," Grandma Lee said to her daughter.

"What message? I didn't get a phone call . . ."

"No, not that kind of message. The kind that gave you the urgent need to come home," Grandma Lee said. "That's why you're here, right?"

Yuna looked surprised at her words. "What do you mean? What's going on?"

"Look at your son closely," Grandma Lee said, pushing him gently toward his mother. "You will see that he is better."

Michael smiled and walked over to his mother. "Hi, Mommy," he said. "I'm okay now. Harper helped me."

Yuna was staring at her little boy's face and gave a choked cry. "You seem yourself again."

"He is," Grandma Lee said as she rose to her feet. "All thanks to Harper and her friends!"

Grandma Lee picked up her bag and approached her daughter. "You almost lost your son because of your closed-mindedness. Because you only accept what makes sense to you. But life doesn't work like that, does it, Yuna? That feeling you had just now that made you come racing home, you don't understand it and yet you are here."

"It was mother's intuition," Yuna said defensively.

"Call it whatever you want," Grandma Lee said. "But you have got to start being more open to the unknown, or you will never know your children."

"What am I missing?" Yuna asked.

Harper walked over to her mother and said, "Mom, remember what happened to me at Briarly?"

Yuna shuddered, her face turning tragic. "Yes . . . was it something like that with Michael?"

Harper nodded. "Yes, Mom. But it's over now."

Yuna looked down at Michael's little face and kissed it. Then she reached over and hugged Harper hard. She looked up to see Dayo standing by herself.

"Dayo, you witnessed this, too?" Yuna asked cautiously.

Dayo threw her arms up into the air and then plopped them down on top of her head. "I don't know what happened, but it was incredible! I've never been so scared in my entire life!" The huge smile on her face was at odds with her words. Harper ran back to hug her friend.

"And you were so brave!"

Yuna still looked confused, but she smiled at the peace that now filled her house.

"How about we ask Grandma and Dayo to stay for dinner?" Yuna asked.

"Oh yes!" Michael crowed. "Grandma, you can sit with me at dinner, and you can tell me all your stories!"

"That would be very nice," Grandma Lee said. She reached over to touch her daughter's shoulder. "It really would be."

Yuna's eyes were watery, but she blinked the tears away and turned to Dayo. "Dayo, will your mother let you stay for dinner?"

Harper laughed to see how confused her friend looked. "If you stay for dinner, I'll explain everything."

Dayo nodded. "I just need to give her a call." As they all walked out the door, Harper heard her grandma ask how Kelly was.

"Her nose is broken and she wants to have plastic surgery to fix it, but otherwise, she's fine," said Yuna.

"Is Kelly gonna hate me forever?" Michael asked.

"Don't be ridiculous! Who could ever hate you?" Grandma Lee responded.

"Do I even want to know about the broken window?" Yuna asked plaintively.

Harper lingered as the others went downstairs. It was nice to see her mom and grandma interacting again. It made her hopeful for the future. Maybe her mom would be more accepting of them both from now on.

After a moment, Rose reappeared.

"We did it," Harper said.

"You did it," Rose replied.

Harper shook her head. "I couldn't have done it without you. You saved me. You always do."

The ghost girl's form shone brightly. "I was so lonely for such a long time. I would have faded into nothingness in my mirror if you hadn't found me again."

Harper felt a rush of affection nearly overwhelm her as she stared at the now familiar pale face and bright-red hair. Here was someone she could always rely on. Always depend upon. How could she have ever forgotten her?

"Thank you for being there for me. For being my friend," she said.

Rose reached over and hugged Harper with a gentle embrace, and Harper felt like she was surrounded by clouds.

"Thank you for being my best friend," Harper continued.

"Always," Rose replied. She let go of Harper with a smile.

And then she disappeared.

HARPER'S STUPID DC JOURNAL

Entry #21

Things I love:

1. *My oldest best friend, Rose.*
2. *My new best friend, Dayo.*
3. *Living close to Grandma Lee*

So I told Dad what was below our basement and he had the architect hire some people to find it. Turns out there was a hidden staircase in the corner of the basement. When they went down there, they found a whole lot of crazy old equipment and notebooks and, of course, the bones of Professor Alfred Mitchell Grady. I didn't see it, but Dad said his skeleton was in perfect condition. Apparently some museum people are interested in taking all the equipment and papers from the basement and attic. My mom wanted to see if we should keep anything ourselves, but I said get rid of it all! And she agreed. We don't need any reminders of Grady in the Raine house anymore.

What I love about being in D.C. is seeing Grandma whenever we want. It's so nice to have her back in our lives. Michael adores her and even Kelly is nicer now. I think she missed Grandma a lot, too. I can see that my mom and grandma are really trying to repair their relationship. If it took fighting off an evil ghost to make that happen, well, it was worth it. Grandma is really good for Mom. She makes her loosen up a little.

And, best of all, Grandma came over today and brought me a special surprise. My very own set of shaman bells and bowls. (Grandma wanted her old set back.) So, it's official. I'm a junior spirit hunter now, and just in time! Dayo told me about the haunted park near school. Rumor has it that people can hear a child crying right before night falls. And little kids complain that when they try to get on the swings, something pushes them off. But no one is there.

Pesky poltergeist or evil ghost? Only one way to find out.

Time to go spirit hunting.

ACKNOWLEDGMENTS

Writing is hard. But it is also deeply rewarding in so many ways. My favorites are the emails, notes, letters, and fan art I receive from readers all over the world. It's when I get to meet readers in person and hear directly from them how much they loved something I wrote. It never gets old. It never gets tired. So my first thank-you is to all my readers out there. Thank you for reading my books. You are all my favorites.

This book wouldn't exist if it wasn't for Alyson Day, my incredible, brilliant, smart, funny, wonderful editor, who teaches me how to be a better writer. Thank you, Aly, for taking a chance on my scary little story.

Thank you to the best assistant editor in the world, Tessa Meischeid, for always being so enthusiastic about Harper's story and also always sending me emails with cool things in them!

Thank you to the Harper art team, associate art director Joel Tippie and artist Matt Rockefeller, for giving me the most amazing covers in the world. I know all the other authors are jealous of me and my beautiful covers. Also, a big thank-you to the rest of my amazing team at HarperCollins: Suzanne

Murphy, Kate Jackson, Kathryn Silsand, Alana Whitman, and Gina Rizzo.

And I wouldn't have a career as a published author if I didn't have the best agent in the industry, Barry Goldblatt, and the awesome Tricia Ready. They make sure I keep panic at bay by calm conversations and yummy treats and 10,000,000% support. Like the best kind of support an author could ever hope for.

I am also so lucky to have some amazing readers who helped me make sure that Harper and Dayo and their world was as authentic as I could get. Thank you to Mike Jung, Martha White, Caroline Richmond, and Elsie Chapman, my first early readers! And all my gratitude and everlasting love to Tracey Baptiste, Nicola Yoon, and Olugbemisola Rhuday Perkovich, who were my final readers. Special thanks to my lovely muse, Adedayo, whom I adore almost as much as her mother! Can we all get together and eat Korean barbecue and Jamaican oxtail stew real soon? I just drooled all over my keyboard.

Speaking of food and drooling, I am so lucky to have my sister, Janet, and my brother-in-law, Laurent, who believe that the best support is love and food. Especially food. Lots of food. Homemade food. Mmmmm. I'm hungry.

Thanks to my mom, who doesn't read my books but is always so proud of me anyway. I love you, Mom!

Thanks to my dog, Tokki, for protecting me from the ghosts that visited while I was writing this book. No thank you for the dog farts. It's okay, I still love you.

Most of all, I want to thank my husband, Sonny, and my kids, Summer, Skye, and Graysin. You are my whole world and my inspiration and my meaning of life and the only people who can make me laugh so hard I pee my pants. But seriously, you guys need to stop that last part, though. I'm running out of clean underwear.